SNOWED IN AT THE RANCH

HOLLY STEVENSON

D0873337

OLIVE LEAF PRESS

For my sister-in-law Julie, thank you for your constant support and encouragement! It means more than you know.

CHAPTER 1

 achel rolled her suitcase through the crowded Kalispell terminal, smiling at the instrumental Christmas music playing in the background. It was a week before Christmas and everyone seemed to be in good spirits. Her stomach fluttered in nervous anticipation as she adjusted the backpack on her shoulder, keeping a firm grip on the camera case she carried in her other hand. She'd stowed it carefully under the seat on the flight from Phoenix, not wanting it out of her sight for one second. The expensive equipment had cost her a small fortune and she couldn't afford to have it damaged or stolen.

She entered the baggage claim, scanning the crowds. Claire Davis, the woman who'd hired her to take promotional pictures and video for Canyon Creek Ranch, had promised Rachel someone would be there to pick her up from her flight. As she glanced around, she didn't see anyone holding a sign with her name on it. She checked her watch. Her flight had landed right on time so someone should be there. The nervous knot in her stomach tightened, but she ignored it. They were probably just running a few minutes late. No big deal. She'd only had a handful of jobs that required traveling since she'd started her free-lance photography business, and she was eager to impress her clients.

But it wasn't like she was the one running late. She needed to calm down.

In an attempt at distraction, she glanced out of the large windows and admired the falling snow outside. It was such a contrast from Phoenix's warm, arid climate. She'd taken a few ski trips to Colorado so this wasn't the first time she'd seen snow, but it still thrilled her to see so much white. Canyon Creek had had an unusually dry winter and her clients wanted to promote the snowmobiling and sleigh rides they offered, so she'd had to wait until the snow fell ... which happened to be the week before Christmas.

Rachel would have preferred not to travel so close to the holidays, but her return flight was scheduled the day before Christmas Eve. She would be home in plenty of time to attend her friend Sage's annual Christmas Eve bash and then to spend Christmas day with her mom.

Best of all, she had an excuse to get away from her ex-boyfriend, Mark. He'd shown up at her apartment last night with a bouquet of roses asking if she wanted to hang out, which was awkward. Rachel had broken up with him weeks before when he'd become increasingly possessive and clingy. She was moving on, and Mark needed to know she wasn't interested in having a relationship with him again. When she'd explained this, he'd been upset, insisting she take the roses and give it some thought. She'd finally taken the bouquet to get him to leave, but she didn't need to give it any more thought. Mark was way too invasive and pushy, and she didn't want to be controlled.

"Excuse me, miss?"

Rachel blinked, jarred from her thoughts when someone tapped her shoulder. A brunette about her age with long wavy hair and wearing a western-styled button-up shirt gave her a tentative look. "Are you Rachel Hartman?" she asked.

Rachel relaxed her shoulders. "Yes. Are you from Canyon Creek?"

She smiled and nodded. "I recognized you from your website. I'm Paisley. My parents own the ranch and asked if I'd come pick you up. I'm sorry I'm late. The roads are pretty slick today."

"No worries." Rachel glanced around the baggage claim, noting that the crowds were thinning out.

"Did you have another bag you're waiting for?" Paisley asked, nodding toward the carousel.

"Nope. Just this," Rachel said, lifting the handles of her roller bag and camera case.

"Can I help you carry anything?" Paisley asked.

"I've got it. Thanks." Rachel gave her a friendly smile to show that she wasn't trying to be rude.

Paisley didn't seem to mind. "Okay. I've got the van parked out front if you want to follow me."

Rachel followed her outside, bracing against the blast of cold air as she left the sliding doors and got hit with the force of Montana winter. "Wow. It's slightly colder here than Phoenix," she said, holding back a shiver.

Paisley laughed. "I can imagine. I've never been to Phoenix before. How long have you lived there?"

"My whole life." Rachel helped Paisley load her luggage into the back of the van.

"The cold might take some getting used to then." Paisley gave her an apologetic smile. "Your coat looks pretty warm though. If you need a hat or gloves or anything like that we have extra at the ranch."

"Thanks. I have some in my suitcase but I think I'll be okay until we get there." She eyed Paisley's shirt. "I can't believe you're not freezing without a coat on."

Paisley shrugged. "I know. My husband Jake is always getting after me about that." She shook her head and gave a wry smile. "Although *he's* one to talk because he forgets his coat half the time too. We both grew up here, so I guess you kind of get used to the cold after a while."

Rachel's eyes widened. She couldn't imagine ever getting used to it, but she knew people felt the same way about the heat in Arizona. She could handle temperatures over a hundred degrees without blinking an eye. Just thinking about the warmth made her shiver. "Is there a heater in the van?" she asked hopefully.

Paisley nodded. "Oh yeah. And a heated seat. Why don't I take your case and you can hop in the passenger seat and get warm?"

Rachel held the camera case to her chest. "I'm actually going to

3

carry this on my lap. It's got my camera in it so I like to keep it with me."

Paisley smiled. "Understood." She closed the back of the van. "Go ahead and climb in. The engines running and the door should be unlocked."

"Thanks." Rachel made her way to the front of the shuttle van, noting the Canyon Creek logo on the side and the heavy-duty looking snow tires before climbing into the passenger seat. She pulled the door closed and found the button for the heated seat before holding her hands up to the heater vents.

Paisley hopped into the driver's side. "So how long have you been doing photography?" she asked as she signaled and pulled away from the curb.

Rachel leaned back into her seat. "I've always loved taking pictures. My mom bought me my first camera when I was in kindergarten so I would stop trying to use hers." She shrugged and lifted her hands. "I don't know what it is, but I've always been drawn to capturing images. As I got older, I earned money for nicer cameras. I played around with the settings and signed up for photography classes. I was totally that geek in high school on the yearbook staff, always wearing a camera around my neck." She laughed at the memory. "I started getting requests to do family photo shoots, and then eventually a few weddings. But those were just side gigs. It wasn't until this past year that I decided to take a crack at freelance photography as a full-time job."

Paisley raised an eyebrow. "That's awesome that you're able to turn your passion into a career. I only had time to glance through your website, but it looked great."

"Thanks." Rachel had worked hard on the website so she appreciated positive feedback.

"How have things been going so far?" Paisley asked.

"The business is going well. I'm starting to pick up more jobs … most of them around Phoenix. I was excited to have the opportunity to travel to Montana for this one. Landscapes are my favorite."

4

Paisley smiled. "Well if there's one thing we've got plenty of at Canyon Creek, it's landscapes."

Rachel laughed and looked out the window. "I can see that. I knew Montana was Big Sky country, but it seems to be big … *everything.*" She shook her head in wonder. "I mean, just look at those mountains. They're massive! How do you not spend all day taking pictures of them?" The snowy peaks towered over Kalispell, and Rachel itched to pull out her camera. But she couldn't do the shots justice through a wet windshield. She would have to be patient.

"I do love these mountains," Paisley agreed. "But I have zero skills when it comes to taking pictures. I don't think I have the patience for it. Neither does Jake. I mean, we take a lot of pictures of our daughter Hannah, but half the time they don't turn out and it's hard to get her to hold still or smile. I feel bad about it." She shook her head. "She's going to grow up and wonder why she doesn't have more cute baby pictures."

Rachel smiled. "I'm sure you do great, but I'd be happy to give you a few pointers and even take some pictures for you if you'd like."

"Really?" Paisley turned to her with a hopeful glimmer in her eyes. "That would be amazing! I'd pay you for it, of course."

Rachel waved a hand. "You don't have to pay me, my second favorite thing to photograph besides landscapes is kids. How old is Hannah?"

"She's almost a year." Paisley's face lit with excitement. "And I would love to capture this milestone. Thanks so much for being willing to help me out."

"Of course." Rachel smiled. "So do you, Jake, and Hannah live at the ranch with your parents?"

"Oh no." Paisley laughed as if the idea were unthinkable. "When we got married my parents gave us a few acres where we built our house. It's far enough away from them to feel like our own place, but close enough to still help out. Jake is a mechanic in town but I work at the ranch a few days a week, mostly driving the shuttle, as you can see. But this week I get to help be your tour guide." She winked. "There's no *way* that Jake and I would live at the ranch. It's crowded enough as it is."

Rachel tilted her head to the side. "That's good though, right? I mean, it sounds like Canyon Creek is getting plenty of business."

"Yes, we've had a fairly steady stream of guests, and we'll have more now that the snow is finally falling. But it's not the guests I'm talking about." Paisley turned to look at her. "I have five brothers, so that's what I meant about crowded."

Rachel's jaw dropped *"Five?"*

Paisley nodded slowly. "And no sisters. So feel free to pity me all you want. There was never a dull moment growing up."

Rachel blinked. "Wow. I can't even imagine what that would be like. I'm an only child, so—" She shrugged and let the sentence hang. Growing up, she'd desperately wanted a younger brother or sister. That longing had intensified with her parents' divorce when she was six. She'd asked Santa for a sibling every Christmas until she finally stopped believing in him. Her friend Sage had helped to fill the void, but to have a whole house full of brothers ... what would that have been like? She felt a mixture of envy and respect for Paisley. "So where do you fit?" she asked.

"My brother Levi and I are the oldest. We're twins," she supplied, glancing at Rachel. "But we don't look that much alike in case you're curious. He's technically older by one minute, which he loves to point out, but I think it's ridiculous." She rolled her eyes and smiled. "Then there's Garrett, Alex, Peter, and Tommy. There's a space between the oldest three and the youngest three, so Tommy is only seven. And he's a rascal, so be warned."

Rachel laughed. "He sounds darling. Do they all live at home?"

"Pretty much. Levi has his own property that my parents gave him around the same time they gave me and Jake ours. Levi's planning to build his house there soon. I think he's ready to get out on his own and away from the chaos, but he does so much work on the ranch that he can't go far."

"I'm sure having so many siblings is helpful when there's a ranch to run," Rachel mused. "The website didn't say how many acres it is, but along with the guest ranch you have cattle too?" Truthfully, Canyon Creek's website only had a few poorly taken photos. Rachel was excited to help remedy that situation for the Davis family. Based on the landscape she'd seen so far, there was huge room for improvement in showcasing Montana's beauty to their potential guests.

"Yep. We stay busy with the cattle and the guests year-round, so like I said, there's never a dull moment. It's all-hands-on-deck in the Davis family. Ranch life is hard work, but I love it." She smiled. "Our parents instilled a good work ethic in us, and along with that they make sure we play just as hard. There aren't many places left where you can live the kind of life we're blessed to live."

"That's beautiful." Rachel thought of her own childhood in the city. The closest she'd ever come to a cow was the dairy section at the grocery store. The farther they drove outside of Kalispell, the more she acknowledged just how much of a city girl she was. The space stretched out for miles here, and she loved it. Her soul felt like it truly had enough room to expand. Giddy anticipation fluttered in her stomach like snowflakes swirling through the air. This was going to be a magical week—she could just feel it.

CHAPTER 2

*L*evi hefted a hay bale onto his shoulder before loading it into the back of the flatbed truck. Small puffs of steam escaped from his mouth into the cold air as he worked. He stripped off his jacket, too warm to keep it on as he loaded the hay. The light snow was turning into thicker flakes and he was grateful to be on his last bale when his mom called out to him from the corner of the barn, holding the hood of her coat to shield her face.

"Levi, has Paisley come back yet?"

He shook his head. "I haven't seen her. Did you try calling?"

"Yes, she left her phone in the kitchen." Claire blew out a breath. "I swear I don't know why she even has one, she's always leaving it someplace." Her forehead creased in concern.

Levi hoisted the last hay bale onto the flatbed and turned to his mom. It wasn't like her to sound irritated. "Is everything all right?"

"Hannah's running a fever." Claire bit her lip. "She hasn't been herself since Paisley dropped her off this morning and I'm worried about her."

Levi straightened. When it came to his niece, he was as protective as a grizzly. "Want me to run her to the clinic in town?" He checked his watch. "Doc Frisby should still be there."

Claire's frown deepened. "I don't know … maybe. Paisley left over an hour and a half ago so she should be coming soon. Let's give it a few more minutes. It's just a fever, so I don't know that we need to panic, but poor little Hannah certainly isn't happy."

"Sounds like she needs some cuddles from her Uncle Levi," he said, stepping in the direction of the house when the unmistakable sound of the shuttle van echoed off of the canyon walls down the road.

Claire's shoulders sagged in relief. "There she is. I've got to get back to the stove, Peter is watching the stew but you know how he is." She raised both eyebrows and pushed a strand of graying brown hair back from her otherwise youthful face.

It never ceased to amaze Levi how well his mom aged, especially considering how hard she worked. But her optimistic outlook seemed to infuse her with energy like an internal solar panel powering her from within. Levi's dad worked hard and took good care of his family and the business, but it was obvious that his mom was the real lifeblood of Canyon Creek Ranch.

"Will you help Rachel get settled and acquainted with the place so Paisley can look after Hannah?"

Levi pushed his cowboy hat up on his forehead. "Sure. Who's Rachel?"

"She's the photographer we hired to take pictures and video of the ranch. You know that marketing stuff Garrett kept talking about? He finally convinced us to hire someone."

"Good for Garrett." Levi nodded. Of all of them, his brother Garrett was the most talented at thinking of ways to improve the business and keep the ranch in the 21st century while maintaining the charms of the old west that their guests sought after. Levi was admittedly more of the "old west" than his twenty-five years belied. He loved working with the cattle and taking the guests on horseback or sleigh rides—though he also didn't mind the horsepower in his snowmobile. But in general, he was content to leave the modern world behind and enjoy the peace of the mountains and rivers of Canyon Creek. He often wondered what he'd done to deserve being blessed to live in the prettiest spot in the world.

"So you're good to help Rachel?" Claire asked, pausing to hear his answer as she headed back toward the house.

"I'm good." He gave her a nod, even though he was already uncomfortable at the thought of showing the woman around. Checking people in and engaging them in friendly conversation was usually Paisley's job. He had no problem guiding guests around on one of the excursions they offered, but that was always with a group. Showing a woman to her guest cabin felt slightly more awkward somehow. Maybe one of his younger brothers would appear and he could rope them into taking over the job.

The shuttle van was fast approaching so Levi adjusted his hat back onto his head and walked quickly toward the main lodge, waving at Paisley as she pulled up to the entrance. He moved to get the passenger side door for the woman he could see sitting there, though the windshield wipers were moving too fast for him to see her clearly. "Welcome to Canyon Creek," he said, arranging a friendly smile on his face. As soon as he got a good look at her his heart skidded to a stop. She was stunning. She tucked a strand of blonde hair away from her cheek and gave him a warm smile that reached all the way up to her deep blue eyes.

"Thank you," she said.

Levi blinked and felt his neck flush as he tried to get his heart to kickstart back to normal. Paisley shot him a knowing grin from the driver's seat. That was the annoying thing about having a twin, she always knew exactly what he was thinking.

"Levi, this is Rachel Hartman. She's staying here for a few days to take pictures of the ranch."

"Nice to meet you, Rachel." He tipped his hat in greeting. "Can I get that case for you?"

"No thanks, I've got it." Rachel pulled the case closer, and Levi wondered if he'd somehow stepped on her toes.

"Rachel, this is my twin brother Levi I was telling you about. See? We don't look that much alike, do we?"

Levi swallowed. They'd been talking about him? What else did Paisley say?

"It's nice to meet you, Levi." Rachel's warm smile snapped him to attention and he held out his hand.

"Careful, it's a little slick," he said, wishing she'd let him take the case for her. His mom had raised him to be a gentleman, and he felt like a slacker standing there while she held it. Would she accept his help getting out of the van or was she one of those women who was offended by the idea?

"Thanks." She took his hand as she stepped down.

As soon as her skin made contact with his, an electric spark shot straight up to Levi's elbow. He made sure Rachel had her footing before letting his hand drop. What was going on with him? It wasn't like they never had pretty guests at the ranch. But while he was friendly, Levi never went beyond professional boundaries. For one thing, it wasn't his place as an employee to overstep that line. And besides that, there really wasn't any point since guests were only there temporarily. Levi wasn't interested in short flings.

"Will you get Rachel's bags out of the back while I check her in?" Paisley asked as she moved around the van.

Levi cleared his throat. "Actually, Mom asked me to check her in. It sounds like Hannah is running a fever so you should go to her."

Paisley's face instantly creased with worry. "A fever? How high?"

Levi gave her a sympathetic look as he shrugged. "I'm not sure. Mom just barely told me, so you go on ahead and I'll look after Rachel." He glanced sideways at Rachel, hoping she wouldn't mind the change in plans.

"Yes, go look after her," Rachel assured her. "I'll be fine."

Paisley nodded. "Thanks. Sorry. I'd just better make sure she's okay."

"Of course."

Levi relaxed, grateful she was understanding. The last thing Paisley needed to worry about was handing off her job. And he had to admit, he didn't mind nearly as much as he had a few minutes ago. Not that he wouldn't have been polite to any guest checking in ... but now he wasn't so anxious to hand the task over to one of his brothers.

11

Paisley waved goodbye before hurrying toward the direction of the house which was set a little apart from the lodge.

"Come on in," Levi said, stepping to get the front door for Rachel. "You can wait in the lobby while I get your bags. Just make yourself at home."

She gave him a faint smile and nodded, stepping into the lobby.

Levi wanted to smack himself as he went to get her luggage. *Make yourself at home? Did people even say that anymore?* He felt uncharacteristically flustered. Okay, so she was gorgeous. So what? Her tan meant she was from somewhere other than Montana—unless she was into those tanning booths or something, in which case she *definitely* wasn't his type and he wouldn't be hers. That zing he'd felt touching her hand was likely just due to the fact that it had been too long since he'd been on a real date. He'd asked Sarah Rupert out to the movies when his friend Brandon had wanted to double last month, but he'd known Sarah forever and they hadn't even held hands. Sarah would never be more than just a friend. Levi rubbed the stubble on his chin as he moved to the back of the van, wondering how long it had been since he'd felt something like that spark from anyone.

Too long.

He retrieved her luggage and closed the van, carrying the roller bag under one arm and the backpack under the other. Rachel opened the door for him.

"Sorry," she apologized. "You can roll that suitcase instead of carrying it. I know it's kind of heavy."

He bit back a chuckle. "I guess I didn't even think about it. When you're used to moving hay bales, this isn't much." He set the suitcase down in the lobby and balanced the backpack on top of it, twisting the strap over the handle so it wouldn't fall. "I'll just get you checked in and then I'll show you to your cabin."

"Sounds good." She glanced around the space, her gaze moving from the large fresh fir decorated near the stone fireplace and then up to the vaulted ceiling. "I think I'll actually take a few pictures of the lobby, if that's all right?"

"Absolutely." Levi smiled and then forced his gaze away, pulling up the information for Rachel's reservation on the computer screen. Her room and board would be covered since his parents were hiring her to help with marketing, but they would have made a reservation to secure her spot during the busy season. He found Rachel's name and nodded in satisfaction when he saw that his mom had booked her in the North Star cabin. The North Star was the nicest of the themed cabins in his opinion. He looked up from the screen. "I've got you checked in, but feel free to take your time. There's no rush."

She'd just pulled the camera from its case and hesitated as she held it at waist-level. "Are you sure? I don't want to keep you. I can always come back and take pictures."

"I don't mind." But maybe *she* minded having him stand there while she worked? "I can give you some space for a while though, if you want?"

Rachel smiled and shook her head. "I don't mind having someone in the room while I take pictures. I'm used to all kinds of distractions." Her cheeks pinked a little and she shifted her weight. "Not that you're a distraction. I just meant that I've photographed weddings and parties and things like that, so I'm used to having people around." She bit the edge of her lip and checked her camera lens, not saying anything else as she turned and began snapping pictures of the room.

Levi pretended to straighten the desk, but his gaze wandered back to Rachel and the *click, click, click* of her camera. She held it with confidence, and he watched in fascination as she framed each shot.

"When did your parents start this ranch?" she asked, not looking away from the fireplace as she took different angles.

He cleared his throat, wondering if she could feel his eyes on her. "My great-grandparents started it actually. Canyon Creek Ranch has been here for over a hundred years. It was just a cattle ranch originally, but about twenty years ago my parents decided to build the lodge and the outlying cabins and turn it into a guest ranch as well. My mom likes having lots of people around, so this is her way of making that happen."

"And your dad? Does he like having guests here too?" She turned to look at him.

"He's definitely more involved in the cattle ranch side of things," Levi admitted. "It was an adjustment for him to get used to the idea of the guest ranch, but he's happy with whatever makes my mom happy."

She smiled and tipped her head. "That's sweet."

He nodded. "Yeah, she's definitely got him wrapped around her finger. But he's used to the guest ranch now and he likes interacting with the people who come to stay. He's in Texas helping my uncle with a cattle drive, but growing up here, he hasn't had many opportunities to travel, so now he says he gets to experience more of the world through the people who visit the ranch."

"That's a nice way to think of it," Rachel said, her smile deepening.

Dang, she had a nice smile. The whiteness of her teeth contrasted with her tan skin, making the effect almost dazzling. Levi looked away, straightening a stack of papers on the desk in an attempt to slow his accelerating pulse. "How about you? Do you travel much for your work?" He glanced up at her again.

"Not as much as I'd like to. I'm from Phoenix and the majority of my jobs have been local, but after seeing this place, I hope I'll be able to travel more." She shook her head and took a picture of the sitting area by the oversized front windows, checking the screen afterward to view the shot. "I can't get over how magical it is."

Levi's lip twitched. "You've only been here for five minutes."

She lifted a shoulder. "Sometimes it only takes five minutes to know something is magical." She pursed her lips in thought before aiming the camera at him and taking a picture of him standing behind the check-in desk. Levi blinked in surprise and she laughed. "Sorry, I couldn't resist." She lowered the camera. "I hope you don't mind. Your mom said I was fine to take pictures of the family while I'm here to give some of the shots human interest."

"Oh." Levi ran a hand along the back of his neck. "I don't mind, but I'm not sure you'll want to take many pictures of me. I'm not very photogenic."

She checked the screen and shook her head. "I don't agree. I think you could be the poster child for this place." She stepped closer and held the screen out for him to see. "What makes you think you're not photogenic?"

He looked at the picture, relieved to see that he didn't look half bad. He shrugged. "Maybe it's more that I just don't like to be in the spotlight," he conceded.

"I see." She analyzed him for a moment and took a slight step back, lowering the camera. "I don't have to take pictures of you if you don't want to be in them. I definitely don't want to make anyone uncomfortable."

He shook his head, not liking that she'd put more distance between them. "No, it's fine. I mean, I don't know that I want to be the *poster child*." He gave her a teasing smile. "But if I happen to be in a shot you like, feel free to take it. Just don't blame me if it doesn't turn out," he added with a wry smile.

"Deal." Her lip turned up in the corner before she stepped toward her camera case, gently setting the camera back inside. "I think I'm ready to put my things in the cabin now." She looked up at him. "But if you've got stuff to do, I'm sure I can find it on my own if you'll point me in the right direction."

He tipped his head to the side and gave her a teasing smile. "Why do I get the feeling you keep trying to get rid of me?"

Her eyes widened. "I'm not. I just feel bad making you wait for me. I'm sure you have lots of things to do."

Truthfully, he did. But in that moment, there was nothing he wanted more than an excuse to spend a little more time with the pretty photographer.

"Hey, what are you doing at the front desk?" his brother Garrett asked, choosing that inopportune moment to saunter into the lobby. "I thought you were out feeding the livestock." His gaze strayed to Rachel and he stopped dead in his tracks, his mouth parting slightly.

Levi would have laughed if not for the sudden flare of jealousy in his chest.

"Rachel Hartman?" Garrett said, stepping forward and eagerly extending his hand to her. "I'm Garrett. I found your website online and told my parents about you. I had no idea you were coming today or I would have personally come to pick you up from the airport."

Levi barely held back an eye roll.

"Hi, Garrett," Rachel said, accepting his handshake with a warm smile. "I didn't know you were the one responsible for my being here. Thanks for giving me the opportunity."

"Of course. I'm a huge fan of your work." Garrett shook her hand for moments longer than necessary before letting it go.

Levi frowned and shifted his weight. No wonder Garrett had wanted their parents to hire Rachel. He'd probably scoured the internet for the best-looking photographer he could find. Typical Garrett. He'd always been a ladies' man, and with his handsome mug, he didn't have a hard time attracting women to him. Not that Rachel wasn't talented, because she clearly was, but Levi had wondered why they hadn't just hired someone local. Now it was obvious. Garrett was looking at Rachel like a bronc rider looked at his first belt buckle.

Levi cleared his throat. "I was just about to take Rachel to her cabin. Hannah's running a fever so Pais asked if I could get Rachel acquainted with the place."

"I'd be happy to show her around so you can feed the livestock," Garrett said, not looking away from Rachel.

"Thanks, but I've got time." Levi waited until he met his eyes, daring him to argue. Even though Garrett was only two years younger and almost Levi's equal for height and build, he had yet to beat Levi in a wrestling match. Levi could still take him, and he wasn't about to leave his younger brother alone with Rachel. Not that Garrett would try anything inappropriate, but the thought of him flirting with her made Levi uncomfortable. She looked like she could be around his age, and her smile seemed just as bright for him as it was for Levi. And Levi didn't like that one bit.

Garrett sucked in a breath, clearly mulling over Levi's deflection before he shrugged. "Maybe I'll join you. I'd love to chat with Rachel about her photography goals since I'll be the one updating the website." He turned and gave her a hopeful look.

"Aren't you supposed to go to Clearwater to get more paper goods for tomorrow?" Levi pressed, annoyed by his persistence. "You don't want to take too long or the grocery store will be closed. The roads are icy so it will be slow going."

Garrett grimaced, shooting a defeated glare at Levi. "I guess that's true." He turned to Rachel, the glare morphing into a cajoling smile. "Any chance you want to come check out Clearwater with me? There might be something interesting to photograph."

Rachel glanced at Levi. "Oh ... um ..." She hesitated.

"She just drove through Clearwater on her way here," Levi said, shaking his head at Garrett. "Let her get settled before pestering her about taking pictures."

"Oh. Right." Garrett's face fell.

"I'd love to talk about the website another time though," she quickly added.

Levi stared at her. Dang if she wasn't sweet too. He was definitely in trouble. Why couldn't she be like so many gorgeous girls and be too absorbed in herself to care about others' feelings? The kindness made her all the prettier.

Garrett brightened. "Great! Maybe we can chat at dinner tonight. My mom's making her famous stew. You'll love it."

"Sounds amazing." She smiled at him, and Levi felt another twinge of jealousy.

"If you'll just follow me, Rachel, I'll show you to your cabin," he said, picking up her bags again.

"Okay." She waved at Garrett. "It was nice meeting you. Good luck in town."

"I'll see you tonight," he answered, his eyes alight with eagerness. "And I'll be happy to show you more of the ranch if Levi doesn't have time."

Levi gave an inner growl. "I've got time," he said, subtly shaking his head at Garrett as he held the door open for Rachel. Garrett gave him a slow smile in return, his eyes holding the same challenge they did when they circled each other in a wrestling match. Levi smirked back.

Game on, bro.

CHAPTER 3

"*I* cannot believe that places like this exist," Rachel said in awe as she walked side by side with Levi on the way to her cabin. Each of the small cabins were decorated with cheerful white Christmas lights. They looked like a village of gingerbread houses, complete with cozy picture frame windows and chimneys emitting the subtle scent of wood smoke intermixed with the crisp scents of snow and pine. Rachel sucked in a big lungful of the fresh air, wanting to memorize the moment.

Levi looked pleased by her reaction. "It's a pretty great place to live, I have to admit. Maybe even magical." He gave her a sideways smile and she grinned.

"See? I told you. There's just something about this place that almost feels unreal. It's a hidden gem. With some professional pictures and a little marketing, Canyon Creek will really make its place on the map."

Levi's eyes tightened and he smiled faintly before looking away. "That's great."

Rachel bit her lip. "Sorry … did I say something wrong? I thought you guys wanted more business. Isn't that why I'm here?"

He nodded. "Yeah, that's exactly why you're here." He shrugged, still not looking at her.

She couldn't help but notice his strong profile beneath his cowboy hat. He'd put it back on before they went outside, and she hadn't been exaggerating when she'd told him he could be the poster child for Canyon Creek. With his tall frame, broad shoulders, and handsome smile, Levi's picture alone would bring women in droves to the guest ranch. And for some reason that thought didn't sit well with her.

"It's just," he continued, pausing as if to choose his words carefully, "it's kind of a catch twenty-two sometimes. The guest ranch brings in a lot of revenue for us, and I enjoy meeting people from all over. But at the same time, I don't ever want to see this place change, you know?" He huffed a laugh and shook his head. "Garrett claims I'm too old-fashioned, and he's right. I sometimes wonder if I was born in the wrong century. I'd take my horse over a machine any day." He gave her a crooked smile that got her heart pumping fast.

She blinked to center her thoughts and nodded. "I think I understand what you mean. The peacefulness here, the land, the break from the rat race. Those are the things that make Canyon Creek special." She met his eyes. "If I lived here, I wouldn't want it to change either."

He smiled and held her gaze for a moment. Her heart skittered about in her chest before he quickly looked away again.

"This one's your cabin. The North Star." He nodded ahead to the cabin set back in a copse of fir trees.

Rachel wanted to squeal at the sight of the quaint cabin, but she held it in. "I love it!" she exclaimed.

Levi laughed. "It's even better inside." He swung the backpack over his shoulder to free up his hand so he could unlock the door. He gave Rachel the key and then flipped on the lights before holding the door open for her.

She couldn't help it. She gave a tiny squeal as soon as she saw a small Christmas tree in one corner. It filled the space with the fresh scent of pine and was decorated with several stars of all shapes and sizes. The star theme continued throughout the cabin, with a beautiful navy down comforter adorned with tiny silver stars and a plush white throw at the foot of the bed. The theme was enchanting, and tastefully done so that it wasn't overkill. A small fireplace across from the bed completed the effect and Rachel clasped her hands in delight. "I seriously can't believe how charming this is."

Levi smiled and stood back, keeping near the door to allow her some space. "I'm glad you like it," he said.

"I *love* it. It's so cool to have this little cabin all to myself." She shook her head and sighed happily. "I could stay here all winter."

His smile deepened. "Think of all the good pictures you'd be able to take."

A small thrill ran through her at the thought. She could imagine all of the landscape shots she could get if she stayed at Canyon Creek for an entire winter. But it was an impossible idea. The Davises were generous to let her stay here for free while she worked for them, but she definitely couldn't afford to stay in one of the cabins long-term … plus there was the minor detail of her business back home to run. She couldn't stay, but she had to admit, the more she saw of the ranch, the more she fell in love with it.

"Well, I'll leave you to get settled then." Levi moved to close the door.

"Wait," Rachel said, unwilling to analyze why she was reluctant to have him leave.

He paused, his brown eyes searching hers beneath the brim of his hat and her heart climbed into her throat.

"Uh," she stammered, grasping for something to keep him there. Her gaze landed on the fireplace and she moved toward it. "Can you show me how this works? Is there a switch somewhere?" She rubbed at her arms. With the door left open it was getting chilly inside.

"Of course. I'm sorry, I don't usually do guest check in so I forgot about the fireplace." Levi stepped into the room and removed his hat, setting it on the nearby coatrack. He must have noticed her rubbing her arms because he hesitated a moment before closing the door behind him. "I'll get this going for you and it will warm up really quick in here."

Rachel nodded. It was already getting warm in there. As soon as he'd closed the door and they were alone, if felt like the air crackled with new intensity. She caught the faintest hint of leather mixed with something deliciously musky, perhaps his cologne or aftershave, and it caused a stirring in her chest. She swallowed and tried to think of something neutral to say to cut through the palpable tension. "So is this the main source of heat in the cabin?"

"Nope. There's a thermostat over on the wall by the bathroom door." He nodded toward the wall and she followed his line of sight.

"Oh good. And I'm glad to know there's a bathroom. I was worried I might have to use an outhouse."

Levi laughed and shook his head. "I don't imagine we'd have too many returning guests if we made them use an outhouse in December."

"True." She chuckled along with him, enjoying the sound of his rumbling laughter before it died down. He retrieved a lighter from his pocket and crouched to hold it to the pile of logs.

"Oh ... it's not a gas fireplace?" She'd assumed the pile of logs in the hearth were fake, just like every fireplace she'd seen in Phoenix.

"This is the real deal," he said with a smile. "But we don't expect our guests to light it themselves, so anytime you want it lit, just call to the front desk and one of the staff will come take care of it for you."

"Wow. Such service," she said, smiling. Could she request who came to light it? In that case, she just might need to have it lit on a regular basis.

"We aim to please." Levi waited until the flames starting licking at the logs. "That will start warming things up in a second, so you should be all set." He stood and straightened, sliding his hands into the front pockets of his jeans. "Can I get anything else for you?"

She shook her head, fighting a blush. The electric feeling returned, charging the air between them. "I'm good. Thanks so much."

He met her eyes and dipped his chin. "Anytime. Don't hesitate to reach out to us if you need anything. I'm sure Paisley will be getting in touch with you soon since she's your official guide here, but I'll also be available if you need me."

"How will I get a hold of you?" Rachel asked before realizing how forward that sounded. "I mean, if Paisley isn't available."

Levi scratched his eyebrow. "Normally I would tell you to call the front desk. But there's a good chance I won't be around in the lodge since I've got the stock to tend to tonight." He paused and tipped his head to the side. "Maybe I'd better give you my cell number so you can get a hold of me ... just in case." His eyes held hers in question.

Rachel's heart flipped. "Okay." She pulled out her cell and handed it to him so he could type in his number.

Levi's neck slowly flushed above the collar as he typed. "Especially with Hannah not feeling well," he explained. "I'm not sure if Paisley will be available and I'd hate for you to feel neglected."

"Thanks. I might have some questions or need directions some-where, so I appreciate you helping me out," she said, making it sound as businesslike as possible to hide the giddiness she felt. She was here to work. Not to flirt with the handsome cowboy. She had to remember that.

"There you go," he said, handing the phone to her and backing toward the door. "I'd better head out now and feed the livestock. But I should be back in time for dinner, so I'm sure I'll see you then."

"Okay. What time is dinner?" She needed to stop asking questions and let the poor guy go. His neck was still flushed and he was clearly ready to escape.

"Six thirty. Do you think you can find your way back to the lodge all right? I can come get you if not." He reached for his hat and put his hand on the doorknob.

As tempting as that was, she knew he was busy and she didn't want to come across as completely helpless. She shook her head. "Thanks for the offer, but I can find it. I mean, I assume I just take the same path back that we came over on, right?"

He nodded. "You probably noticed them, but there are little hanging lanterns set along the path to guide you. We put them there so we wouldn't have guests wandering off into the woods."

Her eyes widened. "Has that happened before?"

He nodded solemnly. "But only one got eaten by a bear, so it's not so bad."

Rachel's mouth dropped open and Levi's face melted into a grin. "Sorry. That's not funny."

She blew out a breath and gave him a mock glare. "*So* not funny." She pointed at herself. "City girl, remember?"

He nodded, still smiling. "I'll try to keep that in mind." He opened the door, placing the hat over his dark hair. "See you soon, City Girl."

"See you."

He touched the brim of his hat, giving her one last smile before he closed the door behind him.

Rachel let out a long sigh and then put her hands to the sides of her forehead. "Rachel, don't even think about it," she warned herself. "Don't you give it one single thought. You're here to work. Nothing else."

She sighed again and dropped her hands, smiling at the crackling fire that was starting to emit a nice amount of heat. Levi Davis was the stuff cowboy dreams were made of. He was almost *too* perfect, just like everything she'd seen of Canyon Creek so far. Her smile faltered —Mark had seemed perfect too, until she'd gotten to know him better. She had to keep her head on straight and focus on the work she came here to do. Her phone dinged with a text and she checked the message. It was from her friend Sage.

Are you at the ranch yet? How is it?

She smiled and typed a reply. *It's dreamy. I wish you could see it. I'll be sure to send pictures.*

You better! I want to see what a real white Christmas looks like. I miss you and hope you have a fabulous time. There's a new guy in my office I think you'd hit it off with. I'm inviting him to the Christmas Eve party so you can meet him.

Rachel shook her head. Sage was always trying to set her up with someone. She was anxious for Rachel to have a boyfriend so that they could double with her and her boyfriend Brice. *We'll see. I'm not sure I'm up to being set up with anyone just yet.* There was a pause before Sage replied.

Because of Mark? How are you doing with that?

No, not because of Mark. There was no way she was going to admit that it had more to do with a certain brown-eyed cowboy she was becoming infatuated with. Admitting it would only make matters worse. She was there to work. Nothing. Else. *I just want to enjoy the party and not stress about if I hit it off with a guy or not.* That was true and hopefully enough to satisfy Sage.

No need to stress. I won't even make a formal introduction between the two of you. But I'm still inviting him.

Okay. I'm looking forward to the party.

They exchanged a few more texts before Rachel tossed the phone onto her bed and stretched her back, trying not to think about Levi or the fact that she had his number in her phone now. She closed her eyes and pulled in a deep breath, resolving to stay on task and take the best pictures and videos she could for the Davis family. The only problem was, when she breathed in, along with the scent of pine she caught the faintest hint of Levi's cologne still hanging in the air. She exhaled and opened her eyes again, slowly shaking her head.

Putting the handsome cowboy from her mind might just prove harder than she thought.

CHAPTER 4

*L*evi tossed the last hay bale off of the flatbed and then pulled the ties from the bales to free the hay and scatter it around on the snow for the cattle. Feeding the livestock over the winter was a lot of work, and normally it was work he didn't mind, but tonight he kept checking his watch, anxious to be done and get home in time for dinner before Garrett got there. He knew his brother would monopolize Rachel's attention if there wasn't anyone to interfere. Plus, he wanted to be the one to make introductions for Rachel. He hadn't received a text from her yet. He didn't always have reliable cell service out in the fields but he kicked himself for not asking for her number as well.

He'd never offered his personal cell number to a guest before, but he hadn't been able to stop himself. There had been a tangible connection between them and it seemed as if she'd been reluctant for him to leave. When she'd asked how to reach him, he couldn't resist giving her his number. It was a stupid thing to do since now he checked his phone every few seconds to make sure he hadn't missed a text … but the fact that Rachel didn't hesitate when he'd offered his number got his pulse racing. Was she feeling the same connection? Was it even possible when they'd only met this afternoon?

Levi scrubbed a hand down his face. He needed to slow down. It wasn't like him to get all worked up like this, analyzing every word and glance for meaning. Rachel was here to work for them, and she was also a guest. Which meant that she was off limits. Not to mention she lived in Arizona. He shouldn't wonder if there was more behind her friendly smiles, or care if Garrett monopolized her attention. *Garrett.* He checked his watch again and gritted his teeth, heading for the truck. If he hurried, hopefully he would make it to the lodge before Garrett came back from town.

Levi started up the engine and tore out of the field so fast it startled the cows, but he didn't care. He was only thinking of Rachel's best interest. Surely she wouldn't want to be stuck listening to Garrett talk about marketing all night or pressuring her about taking pictures. Levi leaned back into the seat but kept his boot pressed down on the accelerator.

Yes. He was only doing this for Rachel's sake, just like he would look after any other guest. There was nothing more to it than that. He grimaced and pressed the gas a little harder, going as fast as he dared in the snow. He'd driven these fields from the time he was old enough to reach the pedals and he knew his limits. Just like he knew his limits when it came to the guests. He would play it cool with Rachel— friendly and professional. He could do that. But when Levi pulled up to the lodge and saw Garrett's truck parked near the back entrance, he forgot all about playing it cool and swung his truck into the nearest spot he could find. He cut the engine and half-jogged into the lodge, nodding at the guests he passed while scanning for Rachel.

He entered the dining hall and stopped short, his gut sinking in disappointment when he saw that she was already seated at one of the long tables with Garrett beside her. Their backs were to him and there was enough commotion with all of the guests getting food and taking seats that no one had noticed him. Mealtimes were like that at Canyon Creek, slightly noisy and fun. Guests, staff, and the Davis family all ate together in the big room with a great mountain view. Levi normally looked forward to the meals and his mom's good cooking—but he'd suddenly lost his appetite.

Rachel was laughing at something Garrett said and Garrett grinned back, his posture leaning slightly toward her. Levi's jaw set. How had he gotten back from town so fast? He must've driven even faster on the snowy roads than Levi had. Someone tapped him on the back and he turned to see his youngest brother Tommy looking up at him with his earnest brown eyes.

"Mom needs to talk to you. She's in the kitchen."

Levi gave him a small smile and tousled his hair. He had a soft spot for his youngest brother. "All right. Are you on cleanup duty tonight?"

Tommy scrunched his nose and nodded. "Ain't I always?"

Levi chuckled. "It's because you're so good at it." In truth, it was one of the few chores Tommy could be entrusted with that wouldn't cause any damage. He had a penchant for mischief.

Tommy shrugged off the compliment and tilted his head up at Levi. "You feed the livestock yet?"

"Yep. I just got back."

He frowned. "Next time I want to go with you. I like when you do doughnuts in the snow."

Levi bit back a smile and bent down, holding a finger to his lips. "Shh. That was supposed to be our little secret, remember?"

Tommy's eyes widened and he nodded. "I didn't tell anybody."

"Good." Levi straightened and glanced around the dining room. "I don't think you have any dishes to clear yet. Have you eaten?"

He nodded again and pulled on Levi's hand. "You'd better go talk to Mom. I told her I'd come get you."

"Okay." Levi allowed himself to be pulled but cast another quick glance over at Rachel and Garrett. Garrett watched her as she talked, his attention riveted to her every word. Levi was itching to get over there and hear what they were talking about, but he wouldn't make his mom wait. Frustration built in his chest as Tommy yanked on his hand again, but then an idea struck. He pulled his hand free from Tommy's and bent down to his eye level. "Listen, Tommy, how would you like to earn a dollar?"

His brother froze and nodded.

Levi smiled. "All you have to do is go sit by Garrett and that pretty blonde lady he's with. Sit right between them if you can, and just talk to her. I'm sure she'd love to hear about that new colt you've been helping to train."

Tommy looked over to Garrett and Rachel and then back at Levi with a suspicious eyebrow raised. "That's all?"

"Yep." Levi nodded. Once Tommy got talking, that was all it would take.

"That's easy!" Without another word, Tommy took off toward their table and Levi watched just long enough to see him wiggle his way between Rachel and Garrett before he headed for the kitchen. If Garrett turned around and saw him laughing, he'd be busted.

He entered the kitchen and found his mom at the stove, giving directions to Alex and Peter who were helping in the serving line. "Alex, I've got more stew here when that pot gets low. Pete, how're we doing on rolls?" she asked.

"We've still got plenty here," Peter said from the serving counter where guests lined up to get their food.

Levi immediately went to the sink to wash his hands. "How can I help?" he asked, drying his hands before coming to stand beside his mom.

She glanced at him. "Oh good. I sent Tommy to look for you. I wasn't sure if you'd be back from feeding the cows yet." She stirred a large pot of stew while bending down to check the window in the commercial-grade oven below. "These rolls are ready to come out. Will you hand me those oven mitts, please?"

"Sure thing." Levi grabbed the mitts from the nearby peg and handed them to his mom, taking over stirring the stew for her and standing to the side as she pulled the rolls from the oven.

Most of the time they employed extra staff at the ranch to help with meals and cleaning the cabins, but with the holidays fast approaching, many of the staff members had traveled home to be with family. The Davises could manage things without the extra help, but it meant they had to step up their game.

Claire set the rolls on the butcher block island to cool and then took her place back at the stove, giving Levi a grateful nod. "Thanks, sweetheart. Would you mind slicing those brownies and setting them on plates? They should be cooled by now."

"We can use a little more salad, Mom," Peter called from the line.

"On it." She set the spoon down and hurried to the oversized refrigerator to retrieve the salad."

"Want me to stir the stew?" Levi asked.

"It'll be fine for a second. Go ahead with the brownies," Claire instructed.

"Okay." Levi moved to the pans of brownies and began slicing. "Where's Paisley? Is Hannah doing all right?"

"That's what I wanted to talk to you about." Claire filled the salad bowl as she spoke, tossing it with precision before handing it back to Peter. "Hannah's still running a fever so Paisley took her home. If she's not better in the morning, she's going to take her to the clinic. I don't think it's anything to be anxious about, but all the same, it's probably best if we don't plan on Paisley's help for at least a day or two."

"Poor Hannah," Levi said, feeling bad for his niece. He would have to stop by and see her later.

Claire nodded. "I know, sweet little thing. Paisley gave her some medicine so hopefully that will help her rest." She went back to her place at the stove, her movements so practiced they seemed effortless. "Anyway, I need someone to take Rachel around so she can get some good shots of the property and I was going to ask you ... but now that I see how well she and Garrett are getting along," she nodded toward the dining hall, "maybe I should ask him instead."

"No," Levi said, turning so abruptly he nearly knocked the pan of brownies to the floor. His mom and both of his brothers turned to stare at him and he shifted, clearing his throat. "I mean, I'm happy to do it. Garrett can take over for Paisley driving the shuttle and checking people in and I'll help Rachel."

"You're sure you don't mind?" Claire asked, frowning. "I know you've got a lot going on with tending to the cattle and horses, and we've booked a few guide trips I'll need you to lead."

"If he doesn't want to, I can help Rachel," Alex piped up from the serving line before turning to them and lowering his voice. "She's a total hottie." He waggled his eyebrows. "Do you think she has a younger sister?"

"I already asked," Peter interjected. "She's an only child." He shook his head regretfully.

Claire rolled her eyes at Peter. "You're only fourteen and too young to date anyway," she chided before pointing a spoon at Alex. "And even if Rachel *did* have a sister, how would you meet her when she lives in Arizona? There are plenty of pretty girls right here in Clearwater for you to date."

Alex snorted. "Yeah, and now we're seniors and I've known all of them since kindergarten." He wrinkled his nose. "Besides, the distance thing wouldn't be a problem. There's always FaceTime, and I've saved enough money from working here that I could buy her a ticket to come visit."

"*If* she existed, you mean," Peter said with a smirk.

"Exactly. And I wish she did." Alex heaved a sigh and hunched his shoulders before looking back at Levi. "Anyway, like I said, I'd be happy to show Rachel around the place for you. Just let me know."

"Thanks, but I can handle it." Levi gave him a firm nod. Good grief, apparently *all* of his brothers were falling for Rachel. Not that he blamed them. He craned his neck and spotted Tommy engaging her in an animated conversation in the dining hall. That kid could talk, but Rachel didn't seem to mind. Her eyes sparkled as she engaged in the conversation, nodding and giving him her full attention while Garrett sulked at the interruption. Levi grinned. He'd have to give Tommy *two* dollars.

Once he dished up all the brownies on the dessert plates he turned to his mom. "These are ready. What else can I help with?"

"I think that's fine for now," Claire said. "Thanks, honey."

"No problem. I think I'll take a brownie out to Rachel and Tommy." He picked up two plates and started walking out of the kitchen.

"Not one for Garrett?" Claire called.

"He can get his own." Levi glanced over his shoulder at her.

She gave him a shrewd look. "Why do I get the feeling there's going to be another wrestling match between you two soon?" she asked.

He shrugged and held up the plates, feigning innocence. "I only have two hands, Mom."

"Uh huh." She shook her head and turned back to the stove. "Just remember she's a guest here, Levi. Don't you two go turning this into a contest and making her uncomfortable."

"Come on, give me some credit," Levi said. "This isn't a competition. It's exactly because she's a guest that I'm stepping in. Garrett is obviously way too invested. Do you really think he talked you into hiring her for her portfolio?" He watched as his mom's face suddenly went slack as she stared past his shoulder. Levi's blood went cold, sensing someone standing behind him.

"Hi Rachel," Claire said, smiling wide to try to salvage the awkward moment.

"We thought we'd come back here and see if you needed a hand," Garrett said flatly.

"How thoughtful!" Claire gushed, though there was still a worried crease between her brows.

Levi squeezed his eyes shut before finally turning to face Rachel and Garrett. She stood stiffly, rubbing one arm as her face flushed crimson. Garrett was shooting daggers at Levi. Tommy, oblivious to the mood, ran up and tugged on Levi's sleeve.

"Can I have my dollar now?" he asked, holding out his hand.

Garrett's eyes cut to Levi and his jaw clenched.

"Uh. In a little bit," Levi hedged. "I was just bringing out this brownie for you." He handed the plate to Tommy and then straightened, taking a tentative look at Rachel. "This one was for you. Would you like it?"

"Oh, um ... thanks." She stepped forward and took the plate from him, not daring to meet his eyes.

Levi wanted to smack himself. Why had he even said that about her portfolio? It sounded like he didn't think Rachel had any talent at all.

Garrett stepped toward Levi, lowering his voice. "Can I talk to you for a sec?"

Levi cleared his throat. "Sure." He glanced at Rachel, trying to convey an apology with his eyes.

Garrett took a hold of his elbow, squeezing harder than necessary as he guided him toward the back door of the kitchen.

"Rachel, sweetheart, would you mind helping me put these brownies on the counter?" Claire asked.

"I'd be happy to," Rachel answered.

Levi could hear the relief in her voice, and he cringed all over again. Normally it was Garrett or even Alex sticking his foot in his mouth. When had *he* become such a bumbling idiot?

They stepped outside and Garrett closed the door behind them before he folded his arms. "What were you thinking, Levi? Why did you say those things?"

Levi winced. "I'm sorry. I had no idea you guys were standing there."

Garrett snorted. "Obviously." He hooked his thumbs through his belt loops and studied him. "And apparently it's 'obvious that I'm way too invested' in Rachel." He worked his jaw as he waited for Levi's response.

Levi shrugged. "I said I was sorry." He squared his shoulders and put his hands at his waist. "But don't tell me it isn't true. I saw the way you looked at Rachel the moment you saw her." He stared his brother down.

To his surprise, Garrett laughed, the hardness of his expression melting away as he shook his head in amusement. "Man, I never thought I'd see the day."

Levi raised an eyebrow, completely lost. "Excuse me?"

Garett straightened and clapped him on the shoulder. "Look, I admit I was attracted to Rachel. Who wouldn't be? And I won't pretend it wasn't a factor in my choosing her as our photographer. But I'm not too proud to accept defeat either."

Levi frowned. Was he missing something? He'd half expected his brother to take a swing at him and this total one-eighty had his head spinning. "Garrett, what are you talking about?"

"You." He pointed at him and grinned. "You like Rachel."

Levi huffed a laugh. "I barely know her."

"I know. Which is what makes this whole thing so unexpected. I've never seen you jealous before." His eyes danced with mirth. "It's super entertaining."

Levi blew out a loud breath and shook his head. "We're done here." He moved to go back into the kitchen but Garrett blocked his path.

"Wait. Don't you even want to know why I'm admitting defeat?"

"No," Levi growled. "This whole conversation is ridiculous and we have work to do."

"Fine. If you won't ask, I'll just tell you," Garrett persisted. "I was pulling out all the stops with Rachel at dinner, being my usual charming self, but it was obvious she wasn't interested."

"That must have been a real blow to your ego," Levi said dryly. It would do Garrett some good to get turned down once in a while.

"A little," he admitted before tipping his head to the side. "That is until I realized she was interested in *you*."

Levi's heart kicked up a beat. "She told you that?"

He smirked. "She didn't have to. She tried to be subtle about it, but the whole time I was talking to her she kept looking around for someone. I didn't know who it was until she started glancing at the kitchen. Then when she asked if we should offer to help, the pieces clicked into place. She's interested in you." He poked Levi in the chest and gave a self-satisfied smile. "And the fact that you paid Tommy to run interference tells me that the feeling is mutual."

Hope inflated Levi's chest and he wanted to believe Garrett, but at the same time he didn't. Rachel was off-limits, and entertaining thoughts of her wouldn't do him any good. He shifted his weight. "That's a mighty interesting theory, but how do you know she's not interested in Alex?" he asked, barely holding back a smile as he folded his arms and cocked an eyebrow.

Garrett snorted. "Fine. Deny it all you want. But I'm just letting you know that I'm not too big a man to admit when I've lost." He raised both hands and then dropped them, his hazel eyes uncharacteristically serious as he looked at Levi. "Rachel's not just any girl. She's special, and I think you know that. Don't go ruining your chances by being too professional. It'd be good for you to bend the rules once in a while." He turned, not waiting for his brother's response before adding, "It's cold out here, and I want one of those brownies." Without another word he opened the door and headed back into the kitchen.

Levi stood rooted to the spot for several seconds. He and his brothers had never been ones to show much affection. They were pretty rough and tumble, and mostly bonded by brawling and teasing each other, but in that moment, Levi could have hugged Garrett. His younger brother surprised him with his maturity, observations, and advice. Whether or not Levi could actually take that advice was debatable, but he appreciated it all the same. He felt bad for not bringing Garrett a brownie earlier. He had more to learn from him than he realized.

Levi caught the door before it closed and headed back into the kitchen, anxious to see Rachel again. His thoughts and emotions were as tangled as a tumbleweed when it came to the pretty photographer, but one thing was for sure. He had some apologizing to do.

CHAPTER 5

"Mm, these brownies look delicious," a woman said as she came through the line. She looked up at Rachel. "Are we allowed to take two?"

Rachel faltered, but thankfully Peter came to her rescue.

"Take as many as you like," he said. "There's plenty."

The woman smiled and took two of the small plates. "In that case, I may be back for more." She nodded her thanks before heading to her table.

"I don't blame her. After eating one of those, I'm pretty sure I could finish off the whole pan," Rachel teased.

Peter's face flushed adorably each time she spoke to him. "Feel free to take as many as you want," he said, darting a glance at her.

"Thanks." Rachel smiled. Peter was young, but he looked a lot like his oldest brother. *Ugh!* Why did she keep thinking about Levi? She was grateful that Claire had allowed her to help in the serving line to take her mind off of her embarrassment. It had been mortifying to walk into the kitchen and hear Levi talking about her—even more mortifying when he'd implied that the only reason Garrett had recommended her was for her looks. His words stung, but she'd kept her head high. She had a solid portfolio, and if there was one thing she was confident about, it was her photography skills. Levi could question that all he wanted, but when she was finished with her job here, he would see that she was worthy of her hire.

The back door opened and Rachel turned to see Garrett strut into the kitchen. Several seconds later Levi followed behind him. He met her gaze and she quickly turned back to the serving line.

"I can take over for you now, Rachel," Garrett said behind her.

She turned, not daring to look in Levi's direction again. "Are you sure? I really don't mind."

He smiled. "You weren't hired to come work in the kitchen. Levi will show you around the property so you can get a better idea of what you'd like to photograph."

"Oh." A mixture between anxiety and relief flooded her chest and she finally braved a glance at Levi. "Are you sure you have time? I don't want to impose." She forced herself to maintain eye contact with him. She had nothing to apologize for and she would rather show herself around the property than have a guide who thought she wasn't capable.

"It's no imposition," Levi said, holding his hat in his hands as he fixed onto her gaze. "I'd be honored to show you around."

With that one look, she knew he felt bad about what he'd said, and the pleading look in his brown eyes made her heart race. He was even *more* handsome without his hat on, if that were possible. But she wasn't about to go falling at his feet. Not after what he'd said. She would be civil, that was all. She dipped her head in acknowledgement. "Thanks."

Claire turned from the stove and looked between them before nodding at Levi. "There won't be much for her to see outside right now since it's dark, but you can give her a tour of the lodge and even the barn so she'll have an idea. The Prairie Rose room is open tonight so you can show her that one if she'd like to take some pictures." She turned to Rachel. "And we'll have more cabins ready in the morning after check out that you'll be able to photograph. Levi can look at the schedule and keep you updated on which rooms and cabins are available when."

"Excellent. I already took pictures of the North Star before I got settled," Rachel said, smiling at her. "Thanks again for putting me up there. I feel so spoiled."

Claire beamed. "That's our goal. We're happy you're here, Rachel, and we completely trust your trained eye to capture whatever you think will make the ranch look good. You're a very talented photographer, and we're thrilled to have you."

Rachel flushed, pretending not to notice the sideways glance Claire gave Levi at this last part. Rachel forced her smile brighter. "Thanks. I'm excited for this project. The ranch is so picturesque that it won't be hard to make it look good."

"Well, that's sweet of you to say," Claire returned, wiping her hands on a dish towel. "Just let Levi know whatever you need, and he'll take care of you."

Rachel glanced at Levi and he nodded, giving her a charming half-smile as his eyes met hers. "I'm at your disposal."

Her heart skipped but she lifted her chin slightly. "Thank you." She could ignore the fluttery way he made her feel and be professional about this. Besides, now she had something to prove. "I'm ready for a tour whenever you are."

"How about right now?"

"Great."

His smile slipped a little at her clipped tone, and the childish part of her was glad. Let him squirm a bit.

Garrett looked between them and shook his head as he put on a pair of disposable serving gloves. "You two go enjoy yourselves. And Rachel, if you *really* want to boost our marketing, feel free to take as many pictures of me as possible." He gave her a toothy grin as he held his hands up, wiggling his fingers. "I look particularly fetching with these plastic gloves on, and there's even a hairnet in the back closet I can add if we want to take the look over the top."

She laughed and held up her camera, snapping a quick shot of Garrett holding up his gloves. "Deal," she said, lowering the camera as she puckered her brow in thought. "But let's hold off on the hairnet. It might be too attractive for your future guests to handle," she teased.

He shrugged. "Your loss."

Alex, Peter, and Claire laughed, but Levi only looked half-amused as he chuckled at the banter. He pushed up from the counter he'd been leaning against and set his hat on a hook by the door. "Where would you like to start, Rachel?"

"How about the Prairie Rose room?" she suggested since Claire had mentioned it. "I'll wait until daylight for most of the pictures, but depending on the lighting in the room, I think we can make it work right now."

"All right. In that case we'll head back in the direction of the lobby." He motioned for her to move ahead of him.

"Thanks for dinner, everyone. It was delicious," she said before stepping past Levi.

"Our pleasure, sweetheart," Claire answered and the others waved.

Rachel's heart warmed to them. The Davises were such fun and friendly people—with perhaps one exception. She would have put Levi into those categories as well, if she hadn't overheard what he'd said earlier. She glanced at him as they walked toward the lobby but didn't say anything, waiting for him to carry the conversation.

He seemed slightly uncomfortable as he walked beside her. "Were you able to find your way over here without any trouble?" he asked.

"Yes. Garrett actually came to get me, but now that I've taken the path, I'll be able to make my way back and forth without any issue."

"Good." But his expression didn't look very pleased when she'd mentioned Garrett.

They'd just entered the lobby when Tommy came running up to them, his gaze fixed on Levi. "How about now?" he asked.

Levi cast a cautious glance at Rachel before pulling out his wallet. "Okay. Thanks for your help." He handed two dollars to Tommy who took them eagerly.

"Two?" he asked wide-eyed.

"You earned it," Levi said before gently taking him by the shoulders and pointing him back to the dining hall. "Now you'd better get back in there for clean-up duty."

Tommy nodded and ran off without a backward glance.

Rachel raised a questioning eyebrow at Levi. "Has he been helping you with your chores?" she asked.

His neck flushed. "Nah, he just did me a little favor earlier." He cleared his throat. "We'll go this way to the stairs leading to the guest rooms."

She tilted her head but followed him across the lobby. Levi clearly didn't want to expound on what the payment was for. She couldn't help but think of how Tommy had come out of nowhere and squeezed between her and Garrett at dinner, effectively taking over the conversation. Could that have something to do with it? The idea made her feel fluttery again so she pushed it aside ... though she might ask Tommy about it later.

Levi led her down a hallway with a series of doors made of rustic pine before stopping at one labeled The Prairie Rose. "This is one of my mom's favorites," he explained as he undid the lock. "She and my Aunt Beverly decorated most of the rooms, and Paisley helped a bit too." He flipped the lights on and held the door open for her.

Rachel instinctively lifted her camera at the ready as she entered the floral-themed room. Once again it was tasteful without being too much. "It's lovely," she said, stepping back to take a few shots and test the lighting. "Does your Aunt Beverly work here?" she asked as she adjusted the lens. Levi stayed in the doorway, careful to give her space just as he had when he'd let her into her cabin earlier. He seemed nothing if not a gentleman.

"Beverly actually lives in Texas," he answered. "She and my Uncle Glenn own a cattle ranch just outside of Corpus Christi. We don't get to see them or their family as often as we'd like, but we do get together for Christmas every year. This year they're coming here so you might get to meet them."

Rachel smiled. "I'd like that." She turned and took pictures of the canopy bed draped with soft white fabric and the oversized jetted tub. "It's nice that you have so much family to surround you during the holidays. I have to admit I'm a little jealous."

"What's your family like?" he asked.

She looked through the camera lens, keeping her focus on the best way to frame her shots. "I'm an only child. My parents divorced when I was young and I'm close with my mom. My dad lives in Nevada and we try to stay in touch, though there's probably room for improvement."

Levi was quiet for a moment, as if considering her words and weighing how much to pry. "Do you have any Christmas traditions you enjoy?"

Her heart softened, touched that he would choose a different topic to spare her any potential discomfort. "Kind of. My best friend Sage always throws a Christmas Eve party, so that's one tradition. And my mom and I get matching pajamas that we wear on Christmas morning while we open our presents. We eat a big breakfast and watch a Christmas movie together afterwards." She shrugged. "It's not much, but it's our thing, you know?"

"It sounds great." He smiled, his eyes warm.

Rachel's breath hitched and she quickly turned away, almost forgetting that she was supposed to be upset with him. "What about your family? Do you have any special traditions?" she asked while taking a picture of the room from a different angle.

"We have a few."

She lowered her camera and faced him. "Like what?"

He studied her, a slight curve to his mouth. "I don't know if I want to tell you. It might sound a little overboard."

She shook her head. "Okay, now you *really* have to tell me."

He chuckled, the sound low and rumbling in his chest. "Fine, I'll tell you a few."

She arched an eyebrow, waiting for him to continue.

He tucked his hands into his front pockets and leaned against the doorframe. "It starts Christmas Eve morning with a snow cave competition to see who can build the biggest snow cave or fort, followed by an epic snowball fight. Then we have a gingerbread house competition. There's caroling in the great room after Christmas Eve dinner, and a gift exchange where everyone is allowed to open one present. We stay up late playing card games and then we all bundle up and take a midnight sleigh ride." He shrugged and gave her a wry smile. "No one gets much sleep on Christmas Eve, so we usually take a nap at some point after opening presents on Christmas Day."

Rachel stared in disbelief and a deep longing filled her chest. It sounded amazing. She almost wished she weren't leaving so she could experience it—even as an onlooker. "Wow," she said finally. "Is that all?" she teased.

Levi smiled and scratched his eyebrow. "I told you it was a little overboard."

She shook her head. "Only in the best ways. Do the guests participate too?"

"Anyone is welcome to join in. The only parts we reserve just for family are the gift exchange on Christmas Eve and opening gifts on Christmas Day. It would be a little awkward to open gifts in front of the guests, you know?"

"I can see that." She paused, considering for a moment. "You don't mind sharing your holidays with strangers?"

Levi shook his head. "Our guests are family while they're here. My parents have always had a 'the more the merrier' philosophy. I think it's one of the reasons they had so many kids, and also why we get a lot of returning guests. Everyone wants to feel welcome, and that's our goal. It's why we all eat meals together and join the guests in the game room and on excursions and such. We want them to feel like they belong."

Rachel's chest warmed. "That's a beautiful philosophy—" She bit the corner of her lower lip as an idea budded to life. "And I think you've just hit on what the main marketing angle should be for Canyon Creek."

Levi tilted his head. "I have?"

She nodded. "The idea of belonging. Of being part of the family. And with a family like yours, who *wouldn't* want to be a part of it?"

His mouth turned up in the corner. "I'm glad you feel that way."

She blushed. She hadn't meant it to sound like that. She lifted her camera and pretended to check the settings again. "I mean, everyone is so welcoming and friendly." She glanced up at him through her lashes, unable to hold back a little jab. "Most of the time, anyway."

41

Levi's eyes tightened and he ran a hand along the back of his neck. "Rachel, about what you overheard me saying earlier ... I didn't mean for it to sound like that."

She lifted her chin, enjoying his discomfort more than she should. "Like what?" she pressed.

He shifted. "Like the only reason Garrett wanted to hire you was for your looks. I know you're a talented photographer. I only said that because I was worried that he might be pestering you."

Her heart fluttered at the hint that Levi thought she was pretty, but she shook her head. "He wasn't pestering me. I enjoyed talking with him about the website and photography ideas. I'm always open to feedback."

Levi's brow furrowed and he looked down at his hands. "I can arrange for him to show you around the place if you'd prefer it?"

"No," she answered quickly and then swallowed, not wanting to sound too eager. "I'm happy to have you show me around as long as it's not too much trouble?"

His face relaxed and he glanced back at her, his brown eyes holding hers. "It's no trouble."

"Good." Her stomach did a little flip as their gazes locked and that electric current returned to the air. She blinked twice to clear her thoughts and lowered her camera. "I think I've got enough shots in here." She lifted a shoulder. "Where to next?"

He straightened. "The other rooms are all full for now, and it sounds like you wanted to wait for better lighting for the rest of the lodge?"

She nodded. "It will make for better shots if I get them during daylight hours."

"Okay." Levi shifted, his mouth twisting in thought. "I don't know how the lighting will be for taking pictures, but I can show you around the barn if you'd like."

Rachel brightened. She'd been wanting to check out the big red barn since she'd seen it upon her arrival. "I'd love that."

He waited until she left the room before he flipped off the lights and closed the door. "It's just this way if you want to follow me," he said, tipping his head in the direction of the lobby.

"Okay." She caught a whiff of his musky cologne, liking the way it mingled with the scent of fresh pine from the lobby. What was it about this cowboy that had her senses buzzing on overdrive? He hadn't needed to ask twice—Rachel had a feeling she would follow Levi just about anywhere.

CHAPTER 6

*L*evi led Rachel outside, noting the way she drew her shoulders closer to her neck against the falling snow.

"I can't get over how this stuff keeps falling from the sky," she said, tipping her head up to watch the fat flakes as they made their way toward the barn.

He smiled, walking beside her. "I can't imagine a winter *without* snow. Even our unusually dry start to the season this year was strange. But I'm grateful the snow finally came. The farmers were getting worried about their crops."

Her face was still turned up, mesmerized. "Do you do any farming here?" she asked right before she stumbled and let out a small squeal.

Levi caught her arm, helping her steady herself. "Easy there," he teased. "We can stand still for a minute if you want to keep looking up."

Her cheeks turned a pretty pink in the dim lights from the lantern-lit path. "Thanks, but I'm sure you don't want to stand outside watching snow fall," she said with an embarrassed smile as she tucked a strand of blonde hair behind her ear.

"I don't mind. Really." *I'd watch mud dry if it meant standing next to you.* Levi swallowed back the thought. He needed to lighten the moment, so without warning he lowered himself to the ground, lying flat on his back in the snow. "But if you're going to watch snowflakes properly, you need to do it from this vantage point," he said, tapping the heel of her snow boot.

Rachel looked down at him and laughed. "Is that so?"

"Yep."

"You actually want me to lie down in the snow?"

"Uh huh." He grinned up at her.

She held her camera case to her chest, pursing her lips in deliberation for a moment before she shrugged and lay down beside him, holding the case over her chest like a shield.

"That thing looks bullet proof," Levi chided, motioning to the camera case.

"Thankfully it's snow proof," she shot back, turning her head to give him a playful glare. "I can't believe you're making me do this."

Levi's heart caught at the nearness of her face to his. Dang, she got his pulse racing. He tipped his head back to look at the sky. "Tell me this isn't the best way to look at snowflakes," he said, his voice slightly husky.

Rachel obediently tipped her face to the sky, a slow smile spreading across her face. "Okay. You're right," she admitted, watching the snow in awed silence. "It's so peaceful," she said softly as if afraid to break the stillness.

"It is," he agreed. The desire to reach for her hand almost overcame him. If he was going to stick to his resolve to not flirt with guests, he would have to avoid still moments like this with Rachel. As long as he kept moving, he would be okay. He turned his head to look at her again, ignoring the way his stomach flipped at her cute profile. "The other reason you need to watch the snow from this angle, is so you can do this." He scooted over far enough so he could stretch his arms wide and then made a snow angel.

Rachel gasped. "I've always wanted to make one of those!" She moved her arms and legs against the snow and then Levi helped her to stand and observe her handiwork.

"Not bad for your first angel," he said with an approving nod as he dusted the snow off of his pants.

"It's not as good as yours." She frowned as she studied his snow angel. "How did you make yours so tidy?"

He chuckled. "I've had more practice." He dusted the snow off of her shoulders, careful not to touch any lower than her upper back. "Something tells me you're competitive," he teased.

She scrunched her nose and shrugged. "Maybe a little."

"It's too bad you won't be here for our snow fort and gingerbread competitions then." He would have liked to watch her competitive spirit for those activities—and if he were being honest with himself, that wasn't the only reason he wanted her there.

She tipped her head to the side. "How did you know I wouldn't be there? I never told you when I was leaving."

"I checked you in, remember?"

"Oh. Right." The pink in her cheeks deepened and there was a hint of disappointment in her eyes.

Levi's chest warmed at her reaction. Had she been hoping he'd gone out of his way to find out how long she was staying? Because he would have. It mattered to him. More than it should. He cleared his throat. "To answer your question from before: no, we don't farm at Canyon Creek. At least not yet. My parents gave me some land where I plan to build a house and work some crops eventually. My mom grows a massive garden that some might consider farm-worthy, but mostly we're a cattle ranch."

Her shoulders relaxed at the change in subject. "How many cattle do you have?"

"Right now, we've got about five hundred head."

Rachel's eyes widened. "Five hundred?"

He nodded. "It's a full-time job taking care of them. But to tell you the truth, I much prefer taking care of the horses." He slid the barn door open, smiling at the familiar scent of animals and hay as he turned on the lights. This was his favorite place on the ranch. He'd always loved horses and the quiet of the barn. He'd even slept in the loft dozens of times when he was younger. Rachel's face lit with enthusiasm, and he liked the way she wore her emotions on her sleeve.

"This is incredible," she said, setting her case on a nearby bench to retrieve her camera.

"Is the lighting good enough?" he asked, anxious to be helpful.

"It's fine. But I'll probably come back in the daytime too," she said before snapping a few pictures. She checked the screen and made a couple of adjustments, took a few more pictures and nodded. "Yes, these will turn out great."

Levi enjoyed watching Rachel take pictures, it was like seeing the barn through new eyes as she photographed little elements and details he didn't pay attention to, zooming in close to the horseshoes nailed above the stalls before standing back to take pictures of the horses occupying them.

"Do you have your own horse, or do they all belong to the ranch?" She paused from taking pictures to look at him.

"I've got my own. He's over here." He led her down the long row of stalls to the tall black Friesian gelding. "This is Cal," he said, putting his hand through the wide bars to rub the horse's nose. Cal nickered in greeting.

"Cal?" Rachel repeated.

Levi nodded. "Excalibur, to be exact. Cal for short."

"Ah, that suits him," she said. "He looks like he belongs in a jousting tournament carrying a knight on to victory."

Levi smiled. "And yet the poor guy is stuck herding cattle and taking the guests on trail rides all day." He heard a click and turned to Rachel with a raised eyebrow.

She grinned and snapped another picture. "Sorry not sorry," she teased.

He shook his head. "Like I told you, you're welcome to take whatever pictures you want, but if I'm in them, don't blame me if they don't turn out."

"Oh they'll turn out." Her blue eyes sparkled with confidence. "Do you want to see?" She offered the camera to him but Levi held up his hand.

"I'm good." He turned back to Cal, secretly pleased. Of course it was only for marketing, but for some reason he liked the fact that she would have pictures to remember him by when she went back home. Maybe he could talk her into letting him take a picture of her—especially one of her smiling. His pulse kicked up at the thought. It would only be fair, wouldn't it? Considering all the pictures she'd taken of him?

"He's a beautiful horse," Rachel said, lowering her camera but making no move to step closer to the stall.

Levi had guided enough trail rides to know when someone had zero experience with horses. "Do you want to pet him?" he asked.

She shook her head vigorously. "I don't think I'd better."

His lip twitched. "Are you allergic?"

"No." She shifted and a crease formed between her brows. "I just haven't been around horses."

"Ever?" He might have guessed as much based on her posture.

She shook her head.

Levi studied her, deciding on the sanity of the sudden plan that came into his mind. "We can fix that, if you're interested," he offered, his gaze fixed on hers.

She pressed her lips together and nodded slowly. "O-okay."

He smiled and reached for her hand, a burst of sparks coursing through him as she let him take it. "We'll start slow," he said, gently moving her to stand in front of him and guiding her hand through the bars of the stall before placing it on Cal's muzzle.

Rachel's arm stiffened. "He won't bite?"

"No," he assured her. "It's always a good idea to check with the owner before petting a horse you don't know. Some get a little nippy, but our horses have been trained well, and they all have good temperaments. Cal's a big guy, but he's as docile as a kitten." Levi kept his hand on hers until she relaxed, and then he reluctantly pulled away, putting a little distance between them. Standing this close to her was messing with his resolve to keep things professional.

"His nose is so soft, it's like velvet," she said, gently stroking Cal's muzzle.

"See? He's not so scary." Levi smiled, pleased that she looked more relaxed with each passing second.

"Do you ride him often?" she asked.

"Every day. A horse like Cal needs a lot of exercise—" He paused, it was the perfect opening and he couldn't resist. "But unfortunately I didn't have time to take him out today like I normally do."

Rachel turned, frowning. "That's too bad. Doesn't he get bored in here?"

Levi nodded. "I should probably take him out for a quick ride tonight."

She pursed her lips, the crease returning to her brow. "It's not too dark outside?"

He gave her a crooked smile. "Not with the way the moonlight reflects off of the snow. And Cal knows his way around."

She pulled her hand back from the stall and shifted her weight. "Well I think you should take him then. I can find my way back to my cabin, no problem."

"What if I gave you a ride?"

Her eyes darted to his, wide and unblinking. "On *him?*" she asked, jerking her thumb at Cal.

Levi nodded again, unable to hold back a smile as he searched her face. "We could just take it at a nice, easy walk. I promise I'll keep you safe."

Rachel bit her lower lip as conflicting emotions passed across her expression. "You promise he won't go any faster than a walk?" she hedged.

Levi smiled and crossed his heart. "I promise."

She held up her camera. "What about this?"

"I can either carry it or we can put it in a saddle bag." Was she actually going to agree to this? His stomach flipped in hopeful anticipation.

She deliberated for a few more seconds, her blue eyes tight before she finally nodded. "Okay. But let's use the saddle bag for my camera."

He shook his head, holding back a smile. "You don't trust me, do you?"

She gave him a look and put her hands on her hips. "I'm getting on a horse with you. Don't push it, cowboy."

He laughed. "Point taken. I'll get the tack and we'll be ready to go in a bit."

"Sounds good. I'll just put my camera back in its case."

Levi nodded and then headed for the tack room, still smiling as he went. He was definitely looking forward to this horseback ride.

CHAPTER 7

*R*achel watched in fascination as Levi led Cal out of his stall and tied the lead rope to the large brass ring outside the door. He explained every step of tacking up, making the motion look so effortless it was clear he'd done the process countless times before.

Rachel itched to unpack her camera and take pictures of Levi as he worked, but she didn't want to overdo it. While Levi's face was definitely good marketing for the female crowd, the Davis family might get suspicious if he was featured in the majority of the pictures she took. But that didn't stop her from appreciating the way his broad shoulders stretched beneath the western-style button-down shirt he wore, or the angle of his strong jawline as he bent to tighten the cinch on the saddle. She never would have thought she had a thing for cowboys, but she definitely did—at least for one in particular.

He straightened and inspected the saddle, giving it a small wiggle to make sure he'd tightened it enough and that the saddle bag holding the camera case was secure. "That should do it," he said, turning to her. "Are you ready?"

Rachel swallowed. Suddenly the barn felt warm, and she was half tempted to unzip her coat if not for the fact that they would be going outside again. "I guess so," she said timidly, eyeing the stirrup which seemed impossibly high given Cal's impressive stature.

Levi bent down on one knee, cupping his hands. "Here, I'll give you a leg up."

"He won't go anywhere?" she asked nervously.

"He'll stay put," Levi assured her.

"Okay." Rachel took a deep breath, embarrassed to step onto Levi's waiting hands, but he hefted her up as if she were no heavier than a sack of flour. She stuck her foot into the stirrup and held onto the saddle horn, swinging her other leg over the saddle so that she was sitting upright. "I did it!" she exclaimed, thrilled that she'd overcome her fear and was actually sitting on a horse.

Levi beamed. "Look at you, you're basically a cowgirl."

Cal shifted his weight at that moment and Rachel let out a small squeal, clinging onto the saddle horn with both hands.

Levi held onto the reins and covered his mouth with a fist, his shoulders shaking with suppressed laughter.

"What?" Rachel demanded, unable to hold back a smile herself. "This thing moves on its own. How is that not terrifying?"

Levi dropped his hand, his brown eyes still dancing with amusement. "I'm sorry." He cleared his throat. "But if you could have seen your face just then—" The words choked off as he struggled to hold back more laughter.

She rolled her eyes. "Are you going to stand there laughing at me or are you going to join me up here?" she demanded.

He paused and raised both eyebrows. "Oh. I'd planned to just lead you around. You thought I was going to ride with you?"

Her mouth opened as a furious blush heated her cheeks. "Oh … um … I just thought …" *Ugh.* How mortifying! She'd assumed he was going to ride with her, which she had to admit was a big reason she'd agreed to the ride. It was the perfect excuse to wrap her arms around him and hold on tight. But he was going to lead her around like a kid at a petting zoo? She winced inwardly, wanting to dive into the nearest haystack she could find and stay there.

Levi's eyes lit with mischief as he looked up at her with a flirtatious smile. "I'm kidding. I'll only lead you out of the barn so I can close the door behind us, and then I'll climb on."

She glared at him. "You punk," she said, knocking the cowboy hat off his head.

He laughed and bent to retrieve his hat. "I guess I deserve that," he said, his eyes still shining as he straightened and placed it back on his head.

Rachel's heart skipped several beats. Was he flirting with her? If he was, she liked it. That wasn't good in terms of trying not to be attracted to him—but then neither was riding double.

"I'll lead him nice and slow so you can get used to him moving beneath you," he said before tugging on the reins to lead Cal.

Rachel was prepared for the movement this time and didn't squeal when Cal stepped forward, but she still clung to the saddle horn. Levi glanced back at her over his shoulder, giving her a warm smile before facing forward again. Rachel's stomach fluttered. Okay, he was definitely flirting with her and she definitely liked it.

Levi led them out of the barn and closed the door behind them before looping the reins over Cal's neck. "Are you ready for me?" he asked, looking up at her from beneath the brim of his hat.

She swallowed. *No*, her brain warned even as her heart took control of her voice. "Yes."

Levi smiled and in one swift motion he was up and sitting behind her, just behind the saddle. He wrapped his arms in front of her as he held the reins. "Is that all right?" he asked.

She half turned. "Yes, but are you okay to not be sitting in the saddle?" His feet weren't even in the stirrups. He chuckled and the vibration of his chest against her back sent her senses into overdrive.

"I'm good. I've ridden bareback more times than I can count."

She nodded and faced forward again.

"It finally stopped snowing," he commented, nudging Cal forward at a walk.

"Mm-hmm," Rachel managed, too hyperaware of Levi's chest at her back to think clearly. It could have been hailing outside and she wouldn't have noticed. Every nerve ending in her body was tuned in to his proximity.

"We might even get lucky and see some wildlife," he said, his mouth close enough to her ear that it caused a delicious shiver up her spine.

Rachel cleared her throat, desperately trying to rein in her galloping heart. "That would be amazing," she said. "But I don't want to see any wildlife until I have my camera ready. I would hate to miss the shot."

"Or you could just enjoy the moment and not worry about capturing it," he said with a hint of a smile in his voice.

She lifted a shoulder. "That's the photographer's curse. It's hard to not want to take a picture when there's a moment to be captured."

"I guess I can understand that." He paused. "I wouldn't mind capturing this moment, for instance," he said softly.

Her heart climbed into her throat. She turned slightly to look at him, her senses on fire. Their faces nearly touched, and the look in his eyes said he didn't mind one bit. Her mouth went dry as her gaze fell to his lips and then she flushed and looked away.

What was she thinking? There was no way she could kiss Levi. She'd been hired to do a job here, and she couldn't ruin that by kissing the guy hired to show her around the property—on the first night, no less. How would that look to the Davis family? She wouldn't blame them if they asked her to pack her bags and take the next flight out of town. *No.* She had to maintain professional distance from Levi—at least while she was working. It might not do any harm to keep in touch when she got back home, but for now she had to keep her head on straight. She cleared her throat and stiffened her posture, keeping her face forward.

"I don't mind if you want to have Cal go a little faster," she said.

Levi paused as if sensing her shift in tone. "Are you sure? Don't feel pressured on my account."

She shook her head. "I want to see what it feels like to trot. Is that what it's called?" She gripped the saddle horn again, wishing she felt as brave as she sounded.

"Yeah, that's the next fastest gait. I'll pick him up to a trot but let me know if you want to slow down again. Trotting can get a little bouncy if you're not used to it."

Oh great. Rachel clenched her jaw and nodded, bracing herself for the faster motion. Levi clicked his tongue, and Cal instantly picked up into a trot. He tossed his head and snorted, seeming to enjoy the faster pace. Rachel bounced up and down in the saddle but smiled in spite of the slightly jarring motion. "This. Is. Fun." Her words come out halting. Levi chuckled again. She was coming to adore the sound of his laugh.

"If you can relax, it makes it a little easier to move with the horse," he said.

"Okay." She attempted to relax her rigid posture, easing more into the saddle, and it did help a little. "What's the next fastest gait?" she asked between bounces.

"A lope or canter. But we'll have to try that another time." He pointed ahead. "Your cabin is right there."

A mixture between disappointment and relief swirled through her at the sight of her cozy little cabin. Levi slowed Cal back to a walk and then slid off first before holding out his hand to her.

"Thanks, but I think I've got it," she said, choosing to hold onto the saddle horn to dismount because that seemed easier ... and meant less contact with Levi.

He tucked his hands under his biceps. "Do you have your key?"

"Yes, it's in my coat pocket."

He nodded. "I'll get your camera." He moved to the saddle bag while she unlocked the door. Things had cooled off between them, which was for the best. But that didn't mean she had to like it.

"Here you go," he said, handing her the camera case.

"Thanks." She took the handle with a small shrug. "Looks like it made the journey just fine."

He gave her a half smile, but it was more cautious than before and didn't reach his eyes. "I'm pretty sure that case is indestructible."

"I hope so. I'll be putting it to the test over the next few days."

"Yeah." He scratched his eyebrow. "Speaking of which, what are you thinking in terms of what you want to do tomorrow? Garrett and I are taking a big group out snowmobiling in the morning, and I wondered if you'd be interested in coming along. To take pictures, I mean," he hurried to add.

Her cheeks heated. It had almost sounded like a date invitation, and deep down she secretly wanted it to be. Hopefully that would be a possibility in the future when she wasn't working for his family. "That sounds perfect," she said. "I won't be able to take pictures of any guests unless they sign a photo release, but even if they don't, I can still get pictures of you and Garrett and some landscape shots. What time should I be ready?"

"We'll meet in front of the lodge at 10:30 and will head out. We'll have a helmet for you but be sure to dress in snow clothes." He eyed her coat and boots. "Do you have snow pants and a hat and gloves?"

She nodded. "I came prepared for the Montana winter." She'd ordered the best snow gear she could find online, and she wished she were wearing all of it at the moment. She couldn't stop the small shiver that made her tremble, and she had to clench her teeth to stop them from chattering.

Levi gave her a long look. "How about I stoke the fire for you before I go so it stays warm tonight?"

She let out a relieved breath that made a puff of steam in the air. "That would be great. Thanks." She gestured to Cal. "Do you want me to hold his reins while you work on the fire?"

Levi smiled. "He won't go anywhere. See?" He stepped away from the horse and Cal stayed in place, bending his nose down to sniff once at the snow-covered ground.

"What a good boy," Rachel said, stepping over to pat the horse's neck. "Thanks for the ride, buddy. That was definitely a first."

"You did great," Levi said. "Before you know it, you'll be galloping across the field."

She laughed and stepped back, giving Cal one last pat before she followed Levi into the cabin. "I don't know about that. I'm leaving in two days so that would be pretty impressive progress."

He squinted, his smile slipping slightly. "You never know. A lot can happen in two days."

"True." She met his eyes briefly and then turned away, rubbing her arms. "Brrr! It really does get cold here, doesn't it?" she said, grasping for a change of subject. She moved to the door but only closed it halfway, not daring to close it completely as he'd done before. Something had changed between them since then. Something magnetic and palpable and she didn't trust herself.

Levi glanced at the door, his expression unreadable. "I'll make this quick," he said, stooping to the wood bin to add more logs to the dwindling fire. He blew on the embers until they sparked into flames and then stood, dusting off his knees. "That should keep you warm through the night, but don't hesitate to call the front desk when you're ready to have it built up again. That's pretty much Peter's full-time job here. We call him the fire boss." He winked.

Rachel smiled. "I'll keep that in mind." It wasn't Peter she wanted to come stoke the fire, but she kept that thought to herself.

Levi shifted. "Can I get you anything else?" he asked, meeting her eyes with an earnest expression that made her breath catch.

"Um—" she grasped for something, *anything* that she might need that would keep him there a little longer when her phone suddenly rang and broke through the moment. "Sorry," she apologized, quickly pulling the phone from her coat pocket and checking the screen. Her stomach dropped. It was Mark. She quickly silenced it. "I don't need to get that."

Levi cocked an eyebrow. "Are you sure? I'm just leaving so don't feel like you can't take it."

She shook her head. "Really. I don't need to." She slipped the phone back into her pocket. Mark was about the last person she wanted to talk to anyway. Why was he calling her? Hadn't she been clear that she was moving on?

"Okay. Well, if there's nothing else you need, I'll wish you a goodnight," Levi said, moving toward the door.

"Wait," Rachel called and then bit her lip. Why was she stopping him? Was she crazy? She didn't even know what she wanted to say so she folded her arms across her chest, blinking twice. "Thanks for the horseback ride. And for being willing to show me around the ranch."

His lip turned up in one corner as he touched the brim of his cowboy hat. "Anytime, Rachel. Have a good night."

"Good night."

He closed the door and she let out a long sigh. She liked when Levi said her name ... and the way he smiled at her. She tiptoed to the window and peeked out just in time to see him ride off on Cal, his posture tall and straight in the saddle. She gave a tiny squeal and flopped onto the bed. She was definitely falling for the cowboy—her gaze moved to the glittering stars painted across the ceiling and she smiled—falling faster than a shooting star.

CHAPTER 8

"Okay, are there any questions before we head out?" Levi asked, scanning the group around him and trying not to settle his gaze on Rachel like he kept wanting to. He'd just finished giving the basic instructions on how to ride a snowmobile and everyone seemed fairly attentive. They normally only took groups of six at a time, but today there was a party of nine that wanted to ride together, and Rachel made ten, so Garrett was coming along to lend a hand.

A teenage boy near the back spoke up. "Are we allowed to go off trail at all?"

Levi smiled. He would have asked the same question when he was younger. He shook his head. "Unfortunately, with the snow falling like it is today, the visibility isn't great and we wouldn't want anyone to get hurt or lost, so we're asking that you stick with the group and stay on the trails."

The boy looked disappointed but nodded in understanding.

"Any other questions?" Levi asked. When no one else spoke up he continued, "You may have noticed that other paper along with the safety waiver. There's no pressure to sign the photo release, but if you're willing to be included in some pictures, our friend Rachel here is taking marketing photographs for the ranch."

Rachel smiled and waved. "And I'd be happy to take a few individual or group shots for those who would like them," she added.

Her offer was met by sounds of surprise and approval.

Levi winked at her and then turned to the rest of the group. "Once you've got those waivers signed, go ahead and give them to my brother Garrett, and then get your helmets on and we'll be on our way." Papers ruffled as the guests signed the waivers and handed their clipboards to Garrett. Levi stepped over to his brother. "Did we get one for everyone?"

Garrett combed through the papers. "Looks like we're good." He stacked the clipboards. "I'll run these back to the office, but you can let Rachel know that everyone signed the photo release, so she can take whatever shots she wants." He took a step closer to Levi and lowered his voice. "And speaking of taking a shot, how did it go last night?" He waggled his eyebrows. "I saw you two riding double away from the barn."

Levi snorted and shook his head, casting a furtive glance over his shoulder to make sure Rachel was well out of earshot. Thankfully she was a safe distance away, chatting with one of the guests. He turned back to Garrett. "I was just giving her a ride back to her cabin," he said casually. No way was he going to mention the almost kiss that had kept him tossing and turning all night. There had been a tangible moment between them when she'd turned and her face was mere inches from his. He'd almost forgotten himself and would have kissed her, but then she'd suddenly cooled off, all trace of flirting gone. He couldn't understand what he'd done wrong. The way she'd quickly silenced her phone call did make him wonder though.

He sighed, lowering his voice further. "Besides, I think she has a boyfriend."

Garrett frowned. "Did you ask her?"

"No."

Garrett rolled his eyes. "Just ask her. There's no use getting involved if she's already taken."

"There's no use getting involved either way. She's leaving tomorrow and I'll never see her again."

"You've never heard of a long-distance relationship?"

Levi raised both eyebrows. "One that actually worked? Not really."

"What about Owen and Hope?"

He shifted. Garrett had him there. Their cousin from Texas had met his wife while on vacation at a Colorado mountain resort. She was from California and they'd dated long distance until she'd eventually moved out to Corpus Christi to be with him. Levi blew out a breath. "That's different."

Garrett folded his arms. "How? You've dated the girls around here and so far, nothing has really clicked. If you're interested in Rachel why let something like a few measly states stand in your way?" He shook his head. "Heck, if she'd shown any interest in me, I wouldn't have hesitated."

"I know you wouldn't," Levi said dryly. His brother had a penchant for flirting with any pretty single women who stayed at the ranch. But Levi wasn't his brother. "We'd better get going," he said, steering the conversation back to safer territory as he cast another glance at Rachel. She was standing by her snowmobile adjusting her helmet.

"Fine." Garrett sighed and then tapped Levi on the arm with the clipboards, drawing his attention back. "Ask about the boyfriend, okay?"

Levi shrugged. "We'll see."

Garrett shook his head, clearly dissatisfied by that answer before he walked toward the office. Levi toyed with the snow gloves he held in his hands, thinking about Garrett's suggestion before forcing himself to snap out of it. He had work to do. He donned the gloves and his helmet, checking with the group to see if anyone needed assistance. Once they were all ready, he hopped on his snowmobile, waiting for Garrett to return and take up the rear before he revved the engine and pulled away from the lodge. He looked over his shoulder, making sure that everyone was following. He'd half hoped that Rachel would somehow end up near him, but to his dismay, she was at the back of the group, right in front of Garrett. *It's better this way*, he tried to convince himself. *She has work to do too. She can't be distracted by you or your questions.*

61

He swallowed back the disappointment and forced himself into guide-mode, leading the group on the snow packed trail he'd ridden hundreds of times. It would have been monotonous, but the people kept it interesting. There were new guests to meet and interact with on every ride, and he tried his best to put his effort into getting to know them whenever they stopped to take in the scenery. But his attention kept drawing over to Rachel and Garrett who seemed to be getting along just fine. *More* than fine, in fact. Every time he heard Rachel's bubbly laugh his gut twisted in frustration. He wanted to hear what she and Garrett were talking about. Maybe she *was* interested in Garrett. Could that be why she'd cooled off so fast last night?

Argh. Levi was being ridiculous. He needed to stop caring. Now. But when Rachel laughed again, he started up his engine and got the group moving. That would put an end to the chatting and the laughing. He was pathetic. Garrett wasn't flirting with Rachel. His brother was a rascal at times, but Levi knew him well enough to know that he'd been sincere about bowing out yesterday. Still, that didn't mean that *she* wasn't flirting with *him*. And Garrett had made it clear that he wouldn't hesitate to reciprocate if she was interested in him. Levi blew out a frustrated breath. If that was the case, he would have to be the bigger man and try to be happy for his brother, even as his insides twisted in knots just thinking about the two of them together.

The snow finally stopped falling by the time they stopped at their usual halfway mark near the Clearwater river so the guests could take a break and get pictures. Levi chatted with them, answering the typical questions about wildlife and other facts about the area, always aware of Rachel's location as he did. She was busy taking pictures of the guests, as promised. She still hadn't spoken to him directly this morning. Was she avoiding him?

"It's been a good ride so far," Garrett said, coming to stand beside him.

"You and Rachel seem to be chatty," Levi commented.

Garrett looked at him sideways. "Do I detect a hint of jealousy?"

"No." Levi scoffed, working his jaw before curiosity won out. "What have you been talking about?"

Garrett smirked. "I thought you didn't care."

"I never said that. I said I wasn't jealous," Levi returned.

The whining sound of a drone filled the air and they both turned to see Rachel flying it past the group of riders who were smiling and waving.

"Wow. Cool," Garrett said, distracted from the conversation as he made his way over to Rachel.

Oh no you don't. Levi moved through the knee-deep powder, managing to catch up to Garrett before he reached Rachel.

"That's a nice drone," Garrett commented, nodding toward the sky.

Rachel smiled while keeping her focus on the drone's screen. "Thanks. I can put it away now if you're ready to go. I just thought it would be fun to get a few group shots."

"That's a great idea," Levi interjected, desperate to bring himself into the conversation.

"Thanks." Rachel glanced up at him briefly beneath the visor of her helmet. Her blue eyes held an unreadable expression before she focused back on the screen.

That one glance made Levi's heart stutter. Oh he was in trouble. Serious trouble. He was in new territory when it came to Rachel, and it scared him. With other guests he had no problem keeping things professional and maintaining a polite barrier, but Rachel was a whole other story. It was as if she were weaving a spell over him that he didn't know how or even *if* he could escape from.

"I just got an idea," Garrett said. "It's time for us to keep moving, but wouldn't it be amazing to get a moving shot of the group?"

Rachel's eyebrows went up as she began lowering the drone. "Like, while they're riding?"

He nodded. "Exactly."

Levi tipped his head to the side. "That would be cool."

"You could hang out with her while she flies the drone." Garrett said, clearly holding back an impish smile.

Levi pressed his lips together. A few minutes ago he'd been so jealous he could have wrestled into a headlock, but now he wanted to give him a giant bear hug. "That could work," he said casually, his eyes flicking to Rachel for her reaction.

She caught the drone and looked at him. "Are you sure you wouldn't mind? I don't want to hold up the group, but that actually would make for a great video clip." Her expression turned eager.

"It won't hold anyone up," Garrett said. "You ride with Levi and get the shots you need, and I'll keep us moving along."

"We can catch up to them after you've taken the footage," Levi added, anxious for more than marketing reasons for the plan to be carried out.

"Okay. Let me go get my snowmobile and I'll meet up with you," she said without looking at him.

"Need any help?" he asked.

She lifted a hand. "I'm good. Thanks." She turned, picking her way through the tracks to get to her snowmobile.

Levi waited until she was out of earshot before facing Garrett with a raised brow. "See what I mean? She's acting a little strange. I think she'd rather ride with you."

Garrett shook his head and put a hand on Levi's shoulder. "Dude, it's been too long since you've been in the dating game. You're missing all the clues. She's acting awkward because she's into you." He smiled. "And frankly, you're acting the same way."

Levi straightened, ignoring the comment. He already knew he was awkward around Rachel and didn't need his brother to confirm it. "During one of your chats, did you ask her if she had a boyfriend?"

"Nope." He took off his goggles and inspected them, wiping off traces of snow. "If I'm the one to ask, she'll think I'm interested in her. That question needs to come from *you*." He gave Levi a look before putting his goggles back on with a mischievous smile. "You're welcome, by the way."

Levi didn't have to ask what he meant by that. He returned the smile. "I definitely owe you one. Your brilliance is a little scary sometimes."

Garrett tipped his head to the side. "I do come up with good plans, don't I?"

Levi smirked. "And yet you stay so humble. How do you manage it?"

He lifted his hands. "I'm just naturally gifted I guess."

Levi rolled his eyes. "We'll see. Let's hope your plan doesn't backfire." He cast a nervous glance in Rachel's direction. She started her snowmobile and moved slowly toward them.

"Don't let the opportunity go to waste," Garrett said, following Levi's gaze. "Find out about the boyfriend." He patted his shoulder once and then headed toward the rest of the group. "I'll fill them in on what's happening." He glanced at the sky. "We'd better get moving soon so hopefully we can beat this storm."

Levi looked up and nodded. He'd seen enough snowstorms to know that Garrett was right. They wouldn't have much time before the snow would start falling again and visibility would be poor.

Rachel pulled up beside him, letting the engine idle. "I'm ready whenever you are." She gave him a hint of a smile that didn't quite reach her eyes, and his stomach twisted.

"I'm ready." He returned the smile and then headed to his snowmobile. *Garrett, I hope you're right about why she's acting this way,* he thought as he started it up. *Otherwise it's going to be an uncomfortable ride.* He drove over to Rachel as the rest of the group started their machines and slowly followed Garrett along the trail.

"Where do you want to be standing to take the shot?" Levi asked.

"I'm thinking that clearing would be a good vantage point," she said, pointing to a clearing ahead that was just off to the side of the trail.

"Sounds good. Follow me." He pulled away from the group, glancing over his shoulder to make sure that Rachel was following him. She wasn't. He swung his machine around and headed back to her. "Is everything okay?"

She shrugged, giving an embarrassed laugh. "I know it sounds silly, but now that we're leaving the trail, I'm a little nervous to go down that hill."

He looked to the hill leading to the clearing, which he hadn't thought twice about. But to a novice rider, he could see how it would be intimidating. He turned back to her. "How about I hop on there with you and we can come back for my snowmobile after you get the footage?"

"You don't mind?"

"Not at all."

She nodded, eyeing the hill again. "That sounds like a good plan."

Levi parked his snowmobile and she scooted back on the seat of her machine, making room for him.

"Sorry. You must think I'm a total wimp," she apologized.

He shook his head. "No way. You've been doing amazing for your first snowmobile ride." He pulled forward and she tensed behind him. He glanced over. "Don't worry. I won't let you fall off." When she bit her lip he chuckled. "You still don't trust me?"

"It's not that." Her blue eyes tightened behind her goggles and she shook her head. "It's *me* I don't trust."

"You'll be fine. I promise I won't let anything happen to you," he said, holding her gaze a moment before turning back to the handles. They needed to start moving or they would fall behind the group. His heart sped up when she wrapped her arms around his waist and held tight.

Forget the doubts and the awkwardness, he *needed* to know if Rachel had a boyfriend. And if she didn't, maybe Garrett was right ... maybe it wouldn't hurt to break the rules once in a while.

CHAPTER 9

*R*achel couldn't believe she was riding double with Levi for the second time in twenty-four hours. It was like the Fates were determined to test her after she'd vowed to keep things professional with him. She had no one to blame but herself. When Garrett made the suggestion she could have declined. She could have gathered her courage and attempted the hill, but *no*, what had she done? She'd agreed to ride with him with barely a moment's hesitation. She was weak. Pathetic. And as much as she tried to tell herself it was excitement over taking footage of the riders, she wasn't fooling her heart. It fluttered like a bird breaking free of its cage as she held onto Levi, thrilling in being close to him once again.

"Is this too fast?" he asked, glancing at her over his shoulder.

She blinked once before realizing he was talking about the snowmobile. Her cheeks heated beneath her helmet. "No, this is fine."

"Okay. Here comes the hill. I'll take it nice and easy."

"Thanks." She held on a little tighter, her stomach tickling as they glided down the incline. Before she knew it, they were on level ground again, heading for the clearing. "You make this look too easy," she said.

"A few more rides and you'd be tackling all of these hills," he assured her. "I'm going to speed up a bit so we can reach the clearing and set up before the group passes."

"Sounds good." She kept a tight hold on him as he accelerated, feeling a rush of adrenaline as they moved faster. They reached the clearing and Levi slowed down. "How's this spot?" he asked.

"Perfect."

He cut the engine and climbed off of the seat. Rachel moved to follow, but her snow boot caught the edge of the running board and she stumbled. Levi reached out and caught her before she fell in the snow.

"It's okay. I've got you," he said, smiling as he made sure she had her footing again before letting go.

"Thanks." Her heart climbed into her throat. Why did he have to be so darn sweet? It wasn't helping her resolve to keep things professional. But, she argued, Mark had been sweet at first, too. Anyone could be sweet and thoughtful for a few days, not showing their true colors until later. And she might not get a 'later' with Levi. She would go home and he would be here, probably acting just as sweet and charming to the next guest who came along. The thought made her stomach sink, but it helped her to let go of him and focus on her work.

She unpacked the drone from the seat compartment and let it fly, moving it toward the group of approaching riders. She aimed it at the front of the group, taking several different angles until she was satisfied she'd gotten some good clips. She was about to bring the drone back when someone called out and pointed toward the thick forest of trees ahead.

Rachel gasped in delight when she saw a tall bull elk look their direction before darting into the pines. On instinct she pointed the drone the direction the elk had taken, hoping to get video of him.

"It might be tricky to see him in the trees," Levi called over his shoulder.

"True," she agreed, studying the screen. All she could see was the tops of the snow-covered pines. "Oh wait ... I think I see him!" she said excitedly.

"I'll take you closer." He pulled out a handheld radio from his coat pocket. "Hey, Garrett. Rachel is going to try and get some shots of the elk. You guys can keep moving and we'll catch up."

There was a pause before Garrett radioed back. "Good luck. We'll see you in a bit."

"Roger that," Levi answered before putting the radio back in his pocket.

"I won't take long," Rachel promised, not wanting to hold Levi back from the group.

"No worries," he said. "Once you get your shots it won't take us long to catch up to the others."

"Okay, thanks." She kept her focus on the screen, frowning in disappointment. "I think I may have lost him anyway. I'll just bring it back now—" Her words cut off in a gasp when she suddenly lost power to the drone. "Crap."

Levi stopped the snowmobile, turning to her. "What happened?"

"I lost connection with it." Anxiety wrapped around her throat, threatening to strangle her. What had she been thinking? She should have known better than to fly over the thick forest. She might never find her drone now.

Levi pulled up to the edge of the trees and cut the engine, silent for a moment. "I'll find it. You stay here while I go look."

She shook her head. "No, it's my fault. I'll go."

He stepped off the snowmobile. "There's no way I'm letting you go in there alone. I know this territory. I'll be fine. Let me go check it out." He radioed Garrett again. "Hey, there's an issue with Rachel's drone," he said, keeping his tone casual. "We might not be able to catch up to you guys, but don't wait for us."

"Everything okay?" Garrett radioed back.

"Yep. I'll keep you posted."

"Roger."

Levi stowed the radio and looked at her. "I'll be back in a bit."

She shook her head. "Two pairs of eyes are better than one. I'm coming with you."

He regarded her for a moment as if weighing how long he'd have to argue with her, then he looked up at the sky. Rachel followed his gaze. The dark clouds looming didn't look promising. Levi turned back to her, squinting behind his goggles.

"Okay. Just follow my tracks. The snow will be deep."

She nodded, relieved that he wasn't arguing further. She'd lost the drone, and she was going to help find it. She *hoped* they would find it, at least. She wanted to smack herself for not listening to Levi in the first place. He must think she was a complete imbecile for trying to chase after the elk. "I'm sorry," she said as she followed him, stepping into the tracks he left as he forged through the snow that was well over knee-deep.

"Don't worry about it," he said.

"If we don't find it after a few minutes, I'll cut my losses." She winced, thinking just how great those losses would be.

"We'll find it. Have a little faith," he said, turning to her with a crooked smile.

She sucked in a breath and nodded, trying to share his optimism. "I think I took it in that direction," she said, pointing in what felt like the area she'd aimed the drone. "I mostly saw trees, but there was something that looked like an old wooden structure … an outhouse maybe?"

He straightened. "Really? That's great. I know what you're talking about." He changed direction and walked a little faster, raising his legs high to step through the powder.

"Is this part of the ranch property?" she asked, trying to keep up as snowflakes started drifting down around them.

"Yes. My great-grandpa actually built a small cabin close to here when he first settled in the area, which is part of what you saw. He lived in it until he met my great-grandma and he built them the house where my family lives now."

"It's a lovely house," she commented. "I noticed it yesterday. I love the wrap-around porch."

"It's had a few upgrades since it was first built, but thankfully he made it nice and big. Otherwise we wouldn't have fit," he said lightly.

Rachel laughed but it came out breathy. The snow was falling faster now as she continued scanning through the trees, desperately hoping to catch sight of the drone. A branch cracked several yards away and she started. "What was that?"

"Probably that mysterious elk you were chasing after," Levi teased.

She swallowed. "You don't—you don't think it's a bear, do you?" She had a mortal fear of being gobbled up in the wilderness by a grizzly.

He laughed. "I'm pretty sure all the bears are hibernating by now."

"Oh. Right." She cringed inwardly. One more point for making herself sound foolish.

He mercifully changed the subject. "Just out of curiosity ... and I hope it's not rude to ask, but ... how much did that drone cost you?"

Her heart sank. He was losing hope that they'd find it, just as she was. "A bit," she said weakly before clearing her throat and forcing a laugh. "Which is why you'd think I'd be smarter about where I flew it."

"Hey, that was a big elk," he countered. "Anyone would be tempted to get a video of him."

She blew out a breath. "I can't believe I didn't keep closer tabs on the battery. I'm normally really good at paying attention to it."

"There were a lot of distractions," he said, climbing over a large fallen log and then turning back to offer his hand to her.

You can say that again, Rachel thought wryly, deciding to cut herself some slack. Who could focus with this handsome cowboy around? She accepted Levi's help and climbed over the log, her boot slipping on the wet surface. "Whoa!" she squeaked, preparing to fall into the powder on the other side but Levi caught her, pulling her into his arms to prevent the fall.

"Easy. Are you all right?" he asked, looking down at her. He still wore his helmet and goggles, but she could see the concern in his brown eyes.

She laughed self-consciously, her heart pounding at being in his arms. As if the bear comment hadn't been bad enough, now she'd fallen. Twice. "I'm fine." She straightened, taking a slight step back. "I'm just clumsy."

"It's tricky to find your footing in the snow. I wouldn't expect an

Arizona girl to be used to that." He gave her a warm smile that melted her insides.

"Thanks for being patient with me. On multiple levels." She smiled and looked around. The snow was falling faster now. With a plummeting heart, she knew what needed to be done. "We should probably turn back now. I don't think we're going to find it."

"Don't give up just yet. My great-grandpa's property is just ahead. If we don't find it around there, we'll head back."

"Okay." She'd secretly hoped he would be willing to keep looking, but she didn't want to be selfish about it. The tips of her toes were getting cold, even with three layers of socks beneath her snow boots, but the thought of losing the drone kept her going. She followed Levi until they reached a small clearing. The snow continued to fall faster, but she spotted the outhouse structure she'd seen on the drone camera. "That's it," she exclaimed. But Levi was looking in another direction.

"You're right," he said, trudging over toward an old fence. He bent down and reached for something hidden from her view. When he straightened, she saw the drone in his hands.

"You found it!" She ran toward him and threw her arms around him without thinking, their helmets clinking. "Thank you, thank you, thank you."

He laughed. "You're welcome."

She pulled back, embarrassed by her outburst but too relieved to care.

He handed her the drone. "It doesn't look too worse for the wear. The snow must have cushioned its fall."

She inspected it, relief washing through her that everything seemed to be intact. "Thank goodness for the snow," she said.

Levi shrugged. "There are pros and cons to it. It's a good thing you saw that outhouse so we knew which direction to look. With the way the snow is falling now, the drone would have been covered up before long and we wouldn't have found it until spring."

She shuddered at the thought, noticing that the flakes were falling so fast she could hardly see the outhouse anymore. "We should probably head back," she said.

Levi shook his head and pulled out his radio again. "Garrett, do you copy?"

A few seconds passed before the radio crackled with Garrett's voice. "I've got you. We're almost back to the lodge, where are you guys?"

"We're at Grandpa's cabin. We had to find Rachel's drone but the snow is falling fast. I think we might have to hunker down here until this storm passes."

Another few seconds passed. "Roger that. Can you light a fire or do you need us to come get you?"

Levi paused, looking at Rachel before he spoke again. "I've got matches and there should be some wood still stacked inside. I think we'll be fine, but keep the radio on in case. If this doesn't let up before dark, we'll need someone to come get us."

"Roger."

The radio went quiet and she bit her lip. "I'm so sorry. It's my fault we're in this mess."

He shook his head. "No more apologies. You actually did me a favor. I was on dish duty for lunch, so someone else will get to fill in for me."

She appreciated his attempt to make her feel better, but guilt still pricked her insides. "I'll do the dishes for the rest of my stay. It's the least I can do."

He laughed. "Why don't we just focus on getting you warmed up for now?" He motioned to the drone. "Want me to carry that so you can keep your balance better?"

She cringed, acknowledging the fact that she was clumsy. "That's probably a good idea. Thanks."

He took the drone and then tromped a path for her to follow. The snow was so thick, she could only just barely make out the old cabin secluded in trees several paces away. Levi opened the front door which still looked fairly sturdy in spite of the apparent age of the place. He motioned for her to go inside. She stomped off her boots as best she could in the entrance and then removed her helmet, noting that it wasn't any warmer inside than out. "This place is so cool," she managed through chattering teeth as she set the helmet down on an old wooden table and hugged her arms to her chest for warmth.

"I haven't been out here for a while." Levi closed the door behind them, stomping off his boots and setting the drone carefully on the table before he glanced around. "Looks like the place could use some housekeeping." He ran a gloved finger across a worn wooden table. "But it will have to do for now." He took off his helmet and set it aside. "I'll get a fire going."

"Thanks." She shivered again. "Seems like you should be called the fire boss," she teased. "Considering how many fires you keep having to light."

"Peter might have a strong contender," he said, smiling. "But I haven't earned the title yet. Let's hope I can get one going in here." He moved to a wood box set near an old potbellied stove and opened the lid. "We're in luck. Somebody stocked this pretty well." He lifted out a few logs and began arranging them so they fit snugly in the stove before pulling a small matchbook from his coat pocket.

"Do you always carry matches with you?" she asked curiously. She hadn't smelled cigarette smoke on him but that didn't rule the possibility out.

"Yeah. I've been stuck in a few snowstorms over the years while I was out on horseback or snowmobiling. I learned to keep a pack of matches in my coat all the time, just in case."

She stared at him. "Were you ever stuck somewhere alone?"

"Only once." He struck a match and held it to the logs. It died out before he could get the wood to catch. He gave a disappointed grunt and reached into the wood box again, pulling out a piece of old newspaper. "It would have been more impressive if I'd gotten the fire to light without this. Looks like Peter will keep his title after all."

She smiled faintly, still stuck on the fact that this wasn't his first time stranded in a snowstorm. "What did you do when you were stranded alone? Were you outside?"

He waited until the newspaper caught and the flames began

licking at the logs before he straightened. "I crouched under a tree and waited it out. I had a horse with me, so I guess I wasn't technically alone."

"Cal?"

He shook his head. "This was long before Cal."

Her eyes widened. "How old were you?"

"Nine."

Rachel's mouth fell open. "You were nine years old and you survived being caught in a snowstorm all by yourself?" Her mom hadn't even let her walk alone for the few blocks to Sage's house when she was nine.

He shrugged. "That's life on a ranch. You've got to be tough or you're in for some rude awakenings."

"I guess so." She shook her head slowly. "We had very different childhoods."

He cocked an eyebrow and gave her a crooked smile. "What? You didn't have many snowstorms in Phoenix?"

She smirked. "Believe it or not, this is my first."

"The way you're shivering, I never would have guessed." The playful look in his eyes turned to concern. "Here," he shrugged out of his coat and handed it to her. "Put this on and stand close to the fire until you get warmed up."

She hesitated. "Are you sure you don't need it?"

He shook his head. "I was about to take it off anyway." He continued holding it out to her so she accepted it.

"Thanks." She slipped the coat over the one she wore, letting the sleeves hang down over hers. It smelled faintly musky with a hint of leather. It smelled like Levi. If he hadn't been standing there, she would have closed her eyes and taken a long sniff. The scent made her insides fluttery.

"The fire will take a bit to get going, but it's giving off a little heat."

Rachel didn't protest as he gently touched her shoulder, guiding her closer to the stove. She pushed the sleeves of his coat back so she could hold her gloved hands up to the fire, sighing at the faint warmth. It was nice, but not enough heat yet to stave off her shivering. In spite of two coats and all of her snow gear, she was cold to the core. "I'll bet you've never been stranded in the snow with a guest before though," she said, attempting humor through her chattering teeth.

"Nope. This is a first for me." His brow furrowed; all trace of teasing gone as he studied her. "You're freezing."

"Just not ... used ... to the ... cold," she managed.

"I don't think there are any blankets here, but I'll take a look around." He left to search the rooms.

Rachel stayed by the fire, unable to leave the heat source.

Levi returned less than a minute later, shaking his head. "No luck."

"It's ... okay. I'm ... getting warmer."

He met her eyes, unconvinced. "So warm your teeth won't stop chattering?" He frowned and shook his head. "I'm not going to stand by and watch while you shiver like that."

Rachel was about to protest again when he stepped behind her, wrapping his arms around her waist and pressing his chest against her back. Her heart skipped several beats.

"Sorry," he said quietly. "This is one of the quickest ways to warm someone up, so I hope it's not too uncomfortable for you."

She was extremely uncomfortable, but not in the way he meant. Her entire body was alive and the sudden quivering she felt had nothing to do with the cold. "I'm good," she said, trying to force herself to relax. *He's just warming you up. This isn't a romantic moment.* If only her heart would get that memo. She cleared her throat, wracking her brain for something to say, but her mind was blank, all thoughts centered on the handsome cowboy with his arms around her.

"Is there a boyfriend back home that I'll need to apologize to?" he asked lightly.

Her heart raced. Even though he'd asked casually, could there be more behind his question? She laughed faintly. "No boyfriend. And you don't need to apologize for helping me. You're just being chivalrous." He was quiet for a long moment—so long she wondered if she'd said something wrong.

"Can I confess something to you?" he asked, his voice low and slightly husky, causing a small tremor up her spine.

"Sure," she said softly, unable to breathe as the familiar electric charge filled the space around them.

Levi let go of his hold around her waist and she instinctively turned to look at him. He hadn't stepped back and they stood impossibly close. Her heart hammered as he searched her eyes.

"I wasn't just being chivalrous," he admitted, then squinted and ran a hand through his hair. "I mean, I *did* want to help you get warm, but the truth is … I wanted to be closer to you." He dropped his hand and held her gaze.

Rachel's pulse sped up and she swallowed. "You did?"

He nodded slowly, not breaking eye contact.

Her thoughts raced wildly: *He's your employer's son; you won't see him again after you go home; what if he's putting on an act and ends up being like Mark?* All the reasons why this was a bad idea pummeled her, but when she looked into his eyes, her heart turned to liquid in her chest. It was hopeless to pretend. "I want to be close to you too, Levi," she whispered.

His expression deepened with a look of joyous disbelief before he paused, his forehead creased. "I shouldn't have told you that. I work for the ranch and you're a guest here. I shouldn't cross that line." He frowned, pleading with his eyes. "But I can't seem to help myself."

Her heart pounded. She shook her head and looked down at her gloves. "I know. We really shouldn't. I work for your parents, and I have a job to do here. I don't want them to think I'm unprofessional." She bit her lip and glanced up at him through her lashes. "But when I get back home—maybe I can call you?"

His face relaxed and he nodded, arching an eyebrow. "If you don't, I will," he said, giving her a crooked smile. "I need to get your number. I've been wishing I had it ever since last night."

The knowledge that he'd been thinking about her warmed her to her toes. "I'll text you and then you'll have it."

"Deal. But you'll have to wait until we have service again. This is a cellular dead zone, which is why we use the radios."

She pulled her phone from her coat pocket and nodded. "I see what you mean."

"But I'm holding you to it when we get service again," he said, pointing at her. "You'd better send me that text."

"I will." She smiled, her stomach doing a little flip at the look he gave her as he smiled back. The charge in the room ignited again as they stood there and she had to force herself not to look at his lips. Distraction. That's what she needed. She cleared her throat. "Has the snow stopped yet?"

Levi walked to the nearest window and opened the shutters. "It hasn't stopped, but it's coming down lighter now. I think we'll be fine to head back once you're all the way warmed up."

"Okay." There was a twinge of disappointment at that news. She would have loved an excuse to stay in the small cabin with Levi all day long, but it was for the best. With only one day left at the ranch, she had a lot more pictures she needed to take. Aside from that, if she stayed here much longer with him, she knew she wouldn't be able to resist kissing him, and that would only complicate things. For now it was enough to know that his feelings were mutual. It was only a few days ... she could wait that long.

Of course, it would be talking on the phone instead of seeing him in person, which was not nearly the same, but she felt confident they could work out arrangements to see each other again. She was already reluctant to leave Canyon Creek and wouldn't mind another visit. As much as she was enchanted by winter here, she wanted to see it in the other seasons too and could only imagine what picture opportunities there would be in spring, summer, and fall.

Levi's radio crackled, startling Rachel from her thoughts as Garrett's voice came across the speaker.

"Just checking in. How are you guys holding up?" he asked.

Levi gave her a roguish smile that set loose a swarm of butterflies in her stomach before he held the radio to his mouth. "We're doing great. The snow is letting up, so I think we'll be able to head back soon."

"Cool. No rush though. You're not missing out on anything here."

Levi smiled as if at some private joke before answering. "Rachel is just getting warmed up by the fire and then we'll head out. Thanks for checking in."

"Yep. Stay warm."

Levi smiled again and signed off.

Rachel tilted her head at him. "Why do I get the feeling I'm missing something?"

His smile deepened, displaying a dimple she hadn't noticed before. "It's just Garrett. He's hoping you and I are ... connecting."

"*Connecting?*" she repeated with a smirk.

"Yeah." Levi met her eyes, his expression changing from amusement to something else. He cleared his throat and ran a hand through his hair. "Well, I'm getting plenty warm now. I think I'll step outside and cool off for a bit, but feel free to keep warming up by the fire for as long as you like."

"Thanks." She was warm enough, but she let him step outside, needing a moment herself to collect her thoughts. One thing was for sure, if she was going to be professional, she would need to be careful about how much time she spent alone with Levi Davis.

CHAPTER 10

The break in the storm that allowed Levi and Rachel to
return to the lodge was only temporary. The snow came
back with a vengeance that evening. Levi busied himself with his
chores of feeding the horses and cattle, and once that was done, he
started cleaning tack, doing whatever he could to keep himself from
going to find Rachel. Ever since their mutual confessions at the cabin,
it was taking all of his will power to hold back from openly pursuing
her. He wasn't sure how it was possible that she didn't already have a
boyfriend, or that she was interested in a cowboy like him, but he
wasn't going to second guess the situation. He would be patient and
wait until she went home before he acted on his feelings.

A text came through as he was oiling a saddle. His heart leaped
when he saw that it was from Rachel. She'd texted him once earlier
after they'd gotten back from their ride, but it had only said a simple
hi. Now he read the words eagerly.

Dinner is starting. Are you coming?

He set the rag he was using aside to type a reply. *Just cleaning some
tack in the stable. I'll be there soon.*

Ok. I'll wait for you.

He immediately set the saddle aside for later. What kind of gentleman would he be if he made her wait for dinner? He hurried to the lodge and washed up in the kitchen, giving his mom a quick peck on the cheek before heading out to the dining room to find Rachel. He spotted her sitting at a table with some of the guests that had been on the snow-mobile ride. She looked up, her blue eyes sparkling with a smile when she saw him. Levi greeted the guests before turning his attention to her.

"It looks like you haven't eaten yet," he observed, staring at the empty space in front of her. "I'm about to get in line if you want to join me."

"Sure. Thanks." She nodded at the others at the table and walked with him to the serving line.

"What have you been up to since last I saw you?" he asked.

She smiled. "Well, first I took a hot shower to warm up after our adventure today, and then I took some pictures of the lodge and empty guestrooms while the daylight lasted."

He nodded. "Sounds like a productive afternoon."

"It was." Her eyes flicked to his and then away again, a blush dusting her cheeks.

Levi's heart did a somersault. He liked the way she blushed so easily. They got their food and sat with a different table of guests since the ones Rachel had been talking to had finished and left. She seemed to make new friends easily, and the new table of guests from Connecticut warmed to her almost instantly. Levi was content to eat his food and listen to the friendly conversation, inserting a comment or answering a question here or there, but mostly he enjoyed watching Rachel interact with the guests. Even though they were complete strangers to her, she talked with them as if they were already her friends. It was exactly the way the Davis family acted with their guests, and she did it instinctively. She fit well here.

He pushed the thought from his mind, focusing on his plate. He needed to be careful with thoughts like that ... of picturing Rachel here. She would be gone tomorrow and even though they planned to stay connected, he couldn't get ahead of himself. Yet as he heard her laugh and watched how the guests warmed to her, it was hard not to wish she could stay.

"Did we come on the perfect night or what?" His Aunt Beverly's Southern drawl could be heard at the dining hall entrance. "Claire's lasagna is my favorite."

Levi turned with a smile to see her enter with her husband, his Uncle Glenn, his cousins Owen and Cody and their wives, Hope and Ava. His father came in behind the group and the already cheerful mood in the large room grew even brighter with their arrival. Levi turned to Rachel who was also watching the newcomers. "It looks like you'll get to meet some of my family after all," he said, resisting the urge to reach for her hand.

She smiled. "Is this your family from Texas?"

He nodded. "And my dad. Come on, they'll want to meet you." He excused himself to the other guests and stood, waiting for Rachel so they could walk over together. His mom had already escaped from the kitchen for hugs. He grinned as his dad gave his mom a kiss square on the mouth. They were always openly affectionate, which had embarrassed Levi when he was younger, but now he loved it about them.

"My stars, Levi," Beverly gushed, her eyes twinkling as she came to meet him with a warm hug. "Please tell me this gorgeous girl with you is your girlfriend." She pulled away from him and before he could answer, she'd already moved to give Rachel a hug too.

Levi ran a hand through his hair, knowing he should correct his aunt, but at the same time not wanting to because he liked the assumption—a lot.

Rachel seemed a bit surprised but returned the hug, giving Levi an amused look over Beverly's shoulder that made his heart hammer. Judging by her expression it seemed as if she didn't mind the assumption either.

"I'm Rachel," she said, smiling at Beverly as she pulled away. "I've been hired as the photographer to take some promotional pictures for the ranch."

"Oh." Beverly blinked once in surprise before she held a hand over her mouth, hiding a small smile before she dropped it. "I'm sorry, honey. It's just when I saw you two together ..." She let the sentence hang, glancing between them before she straightened, her smile brightening. "Well I'm surely pleased to meet you. This is my husband, Glenn."

Glenn stepped forward and shook Rachel's hand. "It's a pleasure to meet you, Rachel."

"You too." She smiled at him.

"And my son, Cody and his wife Ava. And Owen and his wife Hope," Beverly continued, motioning to the small group behind her before turning to address them. "This is Rachel, she's a photographer hired to come here and take pictures," she explained.

His cousins and their wives waved and offered greetings which she returned before Levi's parents stepped forward. His dad smiled and shook her hand.

"I'm Joe Davis. We're glad to have you here, Rachel. I hope you've enjoyed your stay so far?"

She returned the handshake. "It's been wonderful. Thanks so much for giving me the opportunity. This place is a photographer's dream."

His dad smiled. "Claire tells me you've been busy taking lots of pictures."

"She got some great drone shots during our snowmobile ride today too," Levi added.

"I look forward to seeing them. It's good to see you, son." Joe stepped away from Claire to give Levi a brief hug. "How are the cattle doing?"

"Just fine." Levi knew it was hard for his dad to be away from the ranch for long. When you owned cattle, it was a full-time job.

His dad nodded once. "We rounded up all of Glenn's cattle earlier than expected and decided to come a day early. I'm glad we did." A crease formed between his brows as he looked at Claire. "This snowstorm is quickly turning into a blizzard, so we may need to prepare the guests for a change in their plans. Have you seen the forecast?"

Claire frowned and shook her head. "I haven't had time to think about the weather. Does it look bad?"

Joe shifted and looked at Rachel, clearly not wanting to upset her. Levi knew that look though. The storm would be a big one.

Rachel cleared her throat, glancing between everyone. "Well, it was so nice to meet all of you," she said, nodding at the group. "I'll let you catch up while I go finish dinner."

"I need to finish mine too," Levi quickly added. He nodded at his mom. "It's delicious, by the way. Need any help serving or cleaning up?"

She shook her head. "No, just go enjoy it. You two have had a long day."

Joe raised his eyebrows. "They have?"

Claire nodded. "Yes, they had a small adventure during the guest snowmobile ride, but Levi can tell you about that later. Why don't you and the others get some dinner while it's warm. I've got to get back to my stove." She began herding the group toward the serving line.

Levi turned to Rachel and motioned for her to go first. "We'd better get back to our dinner before its cold."

"Okay." She waved at the group before walking back to the table with him. The other guests who'd been sitting with them had finished and left. "I don't want to pry," she said, pausing as she sat down, "but how bad do you think the storm will be?"

Levi pressed his lips together as he sat next to her, debating how much to say. "I'll have to check the forecast, but based on my dad's expression—pretty bad."

She processed that for a moment as she picked up her fork. "So ... when he said to prepare the guests, what did he mean by that?" Her blue eyes searched his.

He shifted in his seat. They'd had bad storms before when the guests were snowed in and forced to stay at the ranch longer than they'd planned, but never over Christmas. He didn't want to alarm Rachel without knowing the facts first, but he did want her to be prepared. "They may have to start looking at flight schedules to make some changes."

Her brows pulled together.

"We'll be watching it and let everyone know as soon as possible if that happens," he reassured her. "For now, just enjoy your dinner. Like my mom said, you've been through a lot today. You deserve some down time."

She gave him a contemplative look before turning her attention back to her food. "You've been through a lot too, but you don't seem too affected by it."

He shrugged. "I'm used to the cold, and to long days of work on the ranch. I'm not tired."

"Neither am I." She took a bite of salad, glancing at him sideways.

Levi's chest warmed. If he was reading the signals right, it seemed like she was waiting for an invitation of some kind. But after Garrett's comment about how he was missing signals, it made him question himself. He knew for a fact that he needed to keep things professional with her until she wasn't working for them anymore ... but he *was* supposed to be her guide. He paused. "Is there anything else you'd like to photograph after dinner? I'd be happy to escort you wherever you want to go."

The corner of her lip turned up. "Actually, I haven't taken any pictures of the game room yet. Would you mind showing me where it is when we're done with dinner?"

"Not at all." His heart thumped against his ribcage. With all of the signs in the lodge she could have easily found it on her own, so her request meant she wanted to spend more time with him. And the feeling was mutual. The game room was a nice, public place. He couldn't let his feelings get too carried away in there, so it was perfect.

They finished their dinner and headed for the game room. Levi stopped short to find it empty. Normally there were guests playing pool or card games or air hockey. But tonight the room was silent. He scratched his eyebrow and turned to Rachel. "We can come back when there are guests here so you can include them in the shots." *And so I won't be tempted to pull you into my arms right here and now.* Why was it that every time he was alone with her the air felt charged with attraction? She was so irresistible he didn't dare to look at her.

"No, this is fine," she said. "I'll take a few shots without guests and then come back when there are so your parents will have options to choose from for the website."

"Sounds good." He stood back, unable to keep from watching her as she moved about the room taking pictures of the space.

"There's a nice variety of game options," she commented. "Do you spend much time up here?"

"Now and then." He stayed busy with work, but once in a while, he'd come up and play a round of pool with Garrett or one of his other brothers.

"What do you play?" she asked, taking a picture of the room from a wide angle.

"Mostly pool."

She turned to give him a small smile, lowering her camera. "How about it then? Do you have time for a round?"

He swallowed. She had to stop giving him those little flirty smiles or he wouldn't be able to resist kissing her. "Are you sure about this?" he teased. "Peter may be the fire boss, but when it comes to pool, I'm the reigning champ around here."

Rachel lifted her chin, giving him a lofty look. "Is that so?" She shrugged. "Well I'm not afraid of a little challenge." She removed the camera strap from around her neck and set the camera on a nearby card table. "I've got the pictures I need for now, so let's do this."

He grinned. "There's that competitive side I knew you had in you. All right then." He gestured toward the cue sticks racked along the wall. "Choose your weapon."

She stepped forward and picked a cue without hesitation.

Levi raised an eyebrow. "Are you sure you don't want to test out a few first?"

"Nope. I'm good." She chalked the tip of her cue.

He smirked as he grabbed his own cue and chalked. He'd go easy on her. If she was as competitive as she seemed, he didn't want her to resent him. He racked the balls and offered for her to break. She walked to the front of the table, lined up her aim with the cue ball, and struck. Levi's eyes widened as two striped balls sunk into corner pockets.

Rachel straightened. "Looks like I'm stripes," she said, a faint smile curving her lip.

"Looks like it." Levi rested his hands on his cue stick, watching in amusement as she called two more shots and sank each one. He shook his head. "I guess that's what I get for bragging. You failed to mention that you're a pool shark."

"Who's a pool shark?"

Levi turned at the sound of Owen's Texan drawl. He and his wife, Hope, entered the game room holding hands and watching them with interest. Levi pointed at Rachel. "Our photographer here seems to be a woman of many talents. She's killing me at pool."

"Wow, really?" Owen stepped over to give Rachel a high five. "Thank you. I've never been able to beat this rascal."

Rachel blushed. "My dad really likes pool, so I've learned a few things over the years."

"Mind if we watch?" Owen asked. "I would love nothing more than to see someone school this guy."

Levi rolled his eyes. "Thanks, Cuz."

Owen smirked at him.

"Don't feel pressured if you'd rather not have an audience," Hope said, nudging Owen in the side.

"I don't mind." Rachel looked up from where she was lining up her shot to give Levi a smug smile.

He straightened. "I don't mind either." He met her eyes, holding her gaze for a long moment.

She blinked and looked away, taking the shot and missing.

"Oh … tough luck," Levi said, biting back a smile.

She gave him a playful shrug. "Now that we have an audience, I didn't want to bore them by sinking every shot. We should at least make a game out of it."

"Oh ho!" Owen hooted, holding a fist over his mouth. "Rachel, I like your style. You've got to take it easy on Levi here. His fall from the top has been a long time coming, after all."

Levi shook his head with wry smile and pointed the cue stick at his cousin. "That's enough out of you, or I'll have to demand some of that privacy Hope offered."

"Yes, don't listen to him." Hope nodded. "You two just keep playing your game and pretend we're not here." She wrapped her arms around Owen's waist, pulling him close as she smiled up at him. "Right, Owen?"

He put his arm around her shoulder, gazing down at his wife with a look of complete adoration before he kissed the top of her head. "I'll behave."

Levi gave Hope a little bow. "Thank you."

Rachel laughed and then tilted her head. "Hope, this is probably going to sound weird ... but your face looks familiar to me."

"Are you into yoga?" Owen asked.

Rachel's eyes widened. "Oh my goodness! You're Hope from *Mindful Mornings*, aren't you?"

Hope nodded. "Guilty."

Rachel gave a little squeal. "My friend Sage is a huge fan and subscribes to your yoga channel. She's going to die when she finds out I met you."

Hope smiled. "I'm happy to know she's a fan."

"I am too. I mean, I'm not as into yoga as Sage is," Rachel admitted, "but I've loved your videos that I've seen." She smacked her forehead. "I can't believe I didn't recognize you sooner."

Levi was so distracted by Rachel's enthusiasm that he almost forgot it was his turn. He moved around the table to set up his shot, still listening as he bent down and aimed at the solid maroon ball.

"It's okay, I wouldn't expect you to recognize me," Hope assured her. "But thanks so much for the kind words. I'm doing a yoga session tomorrow morning for the lodge guests if you'd like to join," she offered.

Rachel brightened. "Really? I'd love to!"

Levi smiled to himself, waiting for a pause in their conversation before he called his shot, sending the ball into the side pocket he'd aimed for.

"Nice, Levi," Hope said with an encouraging nod.

"Thanks." He straightened, flicking a glance at Rachel. The small crease by her mouth was the only indication she gave him before she resumed her conversation with Hope.

Owen shook his head, giving Levi a playful look of disgust, but true to his word he didn't say anything to taunt him.

"Five ball, corner pocket," Levi called before taking the shot. He let out a small breath of relief when it went in, not waiting before setting up the next one. He missed and Rachel took her turn.

They played the closest game he'd ever played, and more of his family members came to watch until almost all of his family and a few guests were standing by, cheering and placing friendly wagers on who would win. Levi loved the little haughty looks Rachel would toss his way whenever she made a shot, and he didn't even mind when she sank the eight ball, winning the game. The room erupted with cheers. His family was ecstatic, especially his cousins and brothers whom he'd bested so many times.

Levi folded his arms and leaned back against the table as he watched Rachel, her smile bright enough to set the sun to shame as she accepted the hearty congratulations. His stomach did a funny flip, and he knew there was no use fighting it anymore—he was a complete goner when it came to this girl.

CHAPTER 11

*R*achel was overwhelmed by the support of Levi's family as they gave her hugs and high fives. She couldn't stop smiling, not because she'd beat Levi—although that had been fun—but because for the first time in her life, she felt what it would be like to have a big family. And she loved it. A warmth grew inside her as she felt more than welcomed; she felt like she belonged. Was that just the Davis family hospitality, or was it something more?

Levi met her gaze from across the room, giving her a wry smile as he dipped his chin in acknowledgment of her win. Rachel's heart skittered across her chest before she turned to his cousin Cody who was offering his congratulations.

"I never thought I'd see the day when Levi would lose a game of pool," he said, smiling as he shook her hand. "That was fun to watch. You two are pretty evenly matched."

His wife Ava nodded. "Seriously, that was amazing. Way to represent the ladies." She gave her a high five.

"Thanks." Rachel beamed.

"Will you be staying for a few days? I'd love to watch a rematch," Ava said.

"Unfortunately I leave tomorrow." Rachel glanced over at Levi. He caught her eye and moved from his place near the pool table to join them.

"Did you need me?" he asked, his eyes playful.

"They're wondering about a rematch," she said, suppressing a smile. "Do you think you'd be up for that sometime?"

His lip twitched and he scratched his eyebrow. "I don't know. I can only stand so much humiliation in one weekend," he teased.

Cody laughed and Ava turned to Rachel. "It's too bad you have to leave so soon. Where are you from?"

"Phoenix," she returned.

"Oh." Ava's face fell. "I was hoping you were from around here so you and Levi could get together."

Rachel's eyes widened and heat rose to her cheeks.

"For another game, I mean," Ava quickly added.

Cody snorted and covered it up with a small cough. "If you two decide on a rematch before you leave, let us know," he said, ushering his wife away. "This is Ava's first time here so I'm going to show her the stables."

"See you later." Levi said, his mouth curving up in a smile as he turned back to Rachel. "So," he studied her, "apparently you're going to have to give me some pointers for pool."

Her stomach fluttered at the warm look he gave her, but she put a hand to her throat and fluttered her lashes. "What? And help out the competition? I don't think so."

His brown eyes glimmered and he shook his head. "So competitive. What am I going to do with you?"

She swallowed. She could think of one or two things ... she blinked and pushed the desire away, lifting a dismissive shoulder. "A little competition is good for the soul."

"It sure is." His gaze deepened and Rachel's mouth went dry.

He had to stop looking at her like that. The room was still full of people, and his gaze was entirely too ... too ... unnerving. It reached a place inside her she didn't know existed, sending a rush of emotions flurrying through her faster than the falling snow outside.

"Hey, you two pool sharks," Claire said from across the room.

"We're going to start *It's a Wonderful Life* in the theater room soon, if you're interested."

Levi looked at Rachel. "What do you think? I understand if you're too tired. It's been a long day."

The first edges of fatigue did pull at her a little, but there was no way she would pass up the opportunity to sit by Levi in the theater room. She shook her head before turning to smile at Claire. "That sounds great. And I actually need to get some pictures of that room so maybe I can hurry down there before it fills up."

"Perfect." Claire checked her watch. "We're scheduled to start the movie at nine, so you should have time. And that way you and Levi can have your pick of seats." She winked and left the room.

Rachel grabbed her camera from the card table, and she and Levi made their way to the theater room on the bottom floor. Tommy accompanied them and she was grateful for his constant chatter which helped buffer her growing attraction for Levi. But the sweet way Levi interacted with his youngest brother didn't help. He patiently listened as Tommy talked about the model train he was hoping to get for Christmas, giving Rachel amused glances every now and then that warmed her insides like a rich cup of cocoa.

"This is the theater room, Rachel," Tommy said without a break in his running dialogue. "Isn't the screen huge? And all the seats recline too. It's just like the theater in Clearwater, only better because the seats are more comfortable here."

"Wow, it's great," Rachel said, truly impressed by the size of the room. "Tommy, can you do me a favor and flip on all the lights? I'm going to take a few pictures before everyone gets here."

"Sure!" Tommy ran to the wall of switches and flipped them on.

"We have theater lighting in here," Levi commented. "Will it be bright enough?"

Rachel adjusted the lens and nodded. "It's perfect. Nobody wants to sit in a bright movie theater, right?" She clicked several pictures, moving about the room to highlight the stadium seating and the large screen. Guests started wandering in right as she finished.

"Where would you like to sit?" Levi asked.

She glanced around the room. "I'm fine wherever. I don't want to take a good seat away from a guest."

He shook his head. "They're all good seats, and you *are* a guest."

She shrugged and glanced at the seating again. "How about in the back corner?" Even though Levi insisted she was a guest, she was getting a free stay and being paid for her time, so it seemed like the most out-of-the-way spot in the room.

He lifted an eyebrow but nodded. "Sounds good."

"Yeah, that sounds good to me too," Tommy agreed. He ran to the back row and sat down between two seats, patting one on each side. "Rachel why don't you sit in this one and Levi can sit here."

Levi opened his mouth as if to argue, but Rachel beat him to it. "Thanks, Tommy," she said. She really wanted to sit next to Levi, and that was the problem. Without knowing it, Tommy was coming to her rescue. Levi frowned but didn't argue, taking the seat on the other side of Tommy as Rachel took the one by the wall.

More guests filed in, and Rachel glanced at the quickly filling seats in apprehension. "Will there be enough room? I don't have to watch the movie. I'm fine to go back to my cabin."

He shook his head. "As a *guest*, you're going to stay right where you are." He gave her a playfully exasperated look. "We should be fine, but if not, Tommy and I can give up our seats. In fact," he paused, "why don't I slide over and you can sit on my lap, Tommy?"

Tommy sighed. "Okay." He stood and let Levi take his seat before sitting on his lap.

"Are you sure?" Rachel asked. "I really don't mind. I've seen it before."

Levi put his hand on her knee, sending an electric current straight through her. "It's fine. I promise. Just enjoy the movie and let me worry about the seating."

"Alright," she hedged, trying to find her voice as his hand lingered on her knee for another second before he let it drop.

"Popcorn!" Tommy exclaimed as Claire rolled in the popcorn cart.

"Why don't you go get some for Rachel?" Levi suggested.

Tommy hopped off of his lap without another word and headed

for his mom. Levi turned to her. "I guess I should have asked if you wanted some first."

She smiled. "What's a movie without popcorn?"

"Exactly." He held her gaze for a second as the lights dimmed around them.

Rachel faced forward, her heart beating double time as she forced herself to keep her gaze on the screen. The guests got their popcorn and settled in around them, with a handful of empty seats to spare. Tommy returned with two bags of popcorn for Rachel and Levi. "Here you go."

"Thanks so much," Rachel said, tilting her head at him. "Are you going to have some?"

"Yeah, Mom's got some for me." He glanced at the screen and made a face. "I didn't know this was going to be an old movie. I'm gonna go find Owen and Hope and see if they'll play Uno with me."

"Okay, buddy. Thanks for the popcorn," Levi whispered so as not to disturb the guests.

Tommy nodded and moved down the aisle again.

Levi looked at Rachel. "He has a hard time sitting still," he whispered.

She smiled. "I kind of figured," she whispered back. Their eyes locked and the electric charge filled the space between them again as the lights went fully dark. Rachel shifted in her seat and faced the screen, trying to remember how to breathe.

The movie played for several minutes before Levi slowly lifted his hand and rested it, palm up, on the armrest between them. Rachel glanced down at his hand, her heart pounding hard against her ribcage. The magnetic pull was too strong to resist. Holding her breath, she slowly slid her hand in his, her senses igniting as he interlaced their fingers and turned his head slightly to give her a faint smile.

She bit her lip and smiled shyly back before facing the screen again. His hand was warm and strong, and it took several seconds for her heartrate to steady. If holding Levi's hand affected her this powerfully, she couldn't imagine what his kiss would do. He rubbed his thumb across the back of her hand, causing a cascading shiver down her spine. He scooted closer so that their arms touched. Rachel bit her lip, every cell in her body longed to kiss him. No one could see them in the dark theater, and none of Levi's family was here anyway. She had a feeling he would readily accept her kiss. He was mere inches away … she closed her eyes to resist. Where was Tommy when she needed him?

"If you're tired, you can rest your head on my shoulder," Levi said softly.

Rachel blinked her eyes open, realizing he'd misunderstood why she'd had them closed. But his invitation was too enticing to pass up. She smiled. "Thanks." She leaned her head onto his shoulder, relishing the musky scent of his cologne as he moved his arm around her and rested his head on hers. She couldn't breathe, couldn't think as she floated on a cloud of bliss. She could stay like this forever, securely tucked beside Levi as they watched a movie. The warmth of his body soaked into her like drizzled honey, and she found herself drifting off to sleep.

The lights came back on and Rachel woke with a start, lifting her head off of Levi's shoulder.

He chuckled softly, the sound deep in his chest. "Good morning," he teased.

She pressed a hand to her forehead. "I'm sorry. I didn't mean to fall asleep."

"I'm glad you did. You needed it." His eyes danced with warmth. "I'll walk you out to your cabin to make sure you get there safely. I texted Peter a little while ago to ask him to get your fire going, so it should be nice and toasty in there."

"Thank you." She was touched by his thoughtfulness and missed the feel of his arm around her. Now that the lights were on, it was back to keeping a respectful distance. But at least she was leaving tomorrow. Once she was finished with her work here, they would be able to pursue this growing thing between them.

The guests stirred and Rachel and Levi stood, taking their empty bags of popcorn to the trash on their way out of the theater.

"If you want to wait in the lobby, I'll go collect our coats," he said. "Yours is hanging on the coat rack in the dining hall, right?"

"Oh, yes. I forgot I left it there." She smiled, pleased that he'd noticed where she'd left it. "That would be great, thanks." She looked out of the large windows to the swirling snow outside and shivered. "I'm definitely going to want it."

A crease formed between his brows as he nodded. "It's really coming down. I'll be right back."

Rachel admired the cozy lights of the Christmas tree as she waited for him to return. It had been a perfect night and the thought of leaving the next day would have made her sad, if not for the fact that it meant she could be open with Levi about her feelings—even if it meant long distance.

The approaching sound of her phone ringing drew her attention. Levi was carrying her coat and he reached into the pocket for her phone. He extended it to her, his expression unreadable. "Here you go."

"Thanks." She looked at the screen and her stomach dropped. *Ugh.* It was Mark. Again. Why was he calling her? There was nothing more to say to him. She quickly silenced the call and slipped the phone into her back pocket.

"You can take it if you want to," Levi said. "I can give you some privacy."

"No, it's okay." She blushed. "It's not important."

He gave a brief nod and held her coat out for her. She slipped her arms into the sleeves, wishing it was Levi's arms wrapping around her instead. He donned his coat and held his cowboy hat, turning to her with a raised eyebrow.

"Are you ready for this?" he asked, nodding toward the door.

"Yep." She crossed her arms in front of her, already bracing for the wintery blast.

"Here," he stepped closer and gently pulled her hood up over her head. "You'll need this."

Their faces were inches apart and her heart broke into a steady gallop as he locked onto her gaze. Time stood still as he slowly slipped his hand into hers.

"I'll just hold onto you to make sure you don't stumble in the snow."

She nodded, unable to speak. He smiled and opened the door. A frigid blast of air hit them, but Levi blocked the worst of it, donning his hat and tucking her close to his side. Rachel didn't even notice the cold; not when she had a handsome cowboy to keep her warm.

CHAPTER 12

*L*evi didn't linger in Rachel's cabin. He stayed just long enough to make sure the fire would last through the night, and then left as quickly as possible. There was no question that if he'd paused even a fraction of a second, he would have gathered her in his arms and kissed her until he was certain there wasn't a trace of cold left on her perfect lips. It would have been beyond crossing the line of professionalism, but more than that, he couldn't help but wonder about that phone call.

He hadn't meant to pry, but when he'd handed the phone to her, he'd noticed the name on the screen—Mark. Was it the same person who'd called her the other night? She claimed she didn't have a boyfriend, so he'd reasoned maybe Mark was her brother ... until he remembered that she was an only child. Her dad, maybe? But she'd said she didn't have much involvement with him so it seemed unlikely. Levi didn't want to dwell on it because it was none of his business. But whoever Mark was, the fact that he was calling Rachel at eleven-thirty at night gave him pause. Plus, she'd blushed and been quick to silence it. His stomach turned, and he chased the pesky doubts away like a troublesome coyote. Maybe he would bring it up later, but until then, he would enjoy Rachel's company until she had to leave.

He shrugged the collar of his coat higher on his neck as he looked up at the thickly falling snow around him. It was piling up nearly waist-high now. Thankfully someone had cleared the path to the cabins, otherwise the guests wouldn't have been able to make it to and from the lodge. If the storm kept up like this, no one would be leaving Canyon Creek anytime soon. With a guilty twinge, Levi secretly hoped that would be the case. As much as he was anxious for Rachel to be done with her work and leave the ranch so he'd be free to pursue her, he wasn't ready for her to go just yet. He could only imagine the way her smiles would light up a Christmas morning. She obviously already fit in with his family … and maybe he could sneak in another moment to hold her hand. A swelling of desire built up in his chest and he looked up at the sky.

"Keep it coming," he said, smiling before dusting himself off and heading back into the lodge.

His parents were at the front desk, both wearing concerned frowns as they studied the desktop monitor.

"Everything all right?" Levi asked, joining them.

"We just got word that the airport is closed." His dad gave him a loaded glance before returning his attention to the screen.

Levi sucked in a breath. He hadn't expected his wish to be granted so fast and seeing his parents stress made him feel bad for making it … but only a little. A tiny thrill ran through him at the knowledge that Rachel could stay longer.

"I'm notifying our incoming guests of the situation before they start their travel," his mom added, shaking her head. "I hate to disappoint anyone, especially during Christmas."

"It's not your fault," Levi said, giving her a reassuring nod. "Mother Nature has been holding back this year, and now she's decided to let it all loose at once."

Claire chuckled. "I suppose you're right." Her smile quickly faded. "But I dread telling our guests in the morning. I'm sure they all had

Christmas plans back home, so unless this storm miraculously lets up by tomorrow, it's looking like they'll all be spending Christmas here."

"Which isn't the worst fate." Joe put an arm around his wife and gave her a squeeze. "We'll do our best to make it a memorable Christmas for them, sweetheart." He kissed her on the temple and she leaned into him.

"Right," Levi agreed. "And who knows … some of them might even be excited to spend Christmas at the ranch."

His mom eyed him. "Anyone in particular?" she asked in a playfully innocent tone.

Levi fought the smile that threatened to give him away. "Not necessarily," he answered casually. "It just might be fun for some of them to join in on our holiday traditions. Give them a different holiday experience than they've had before."

"Especially if they happen to be from Arizona," his dad quipped with a wink.

Levi shook his head, unable to hide the smile now. He held up his hands. "I don't know what you're talking about."

"Uh huh." Claire nudged him in the side. "She's a cutie, Levi. The two of you seem to be getting along quite well."

"Just doing my job," he said, forcing back the smile as he cleared his throat and scratched his eyebrow. "Is there anything I can help you with tonight?"

"No, you go on to bed. You've had a long day and you'll be back at it tomorrow," his mom said. "You'll have to get an early start to get the livestock fed so you can be back in time for the snow fort competition. Cody and Owen were already doing some smack talk about how their forts will be the best."

Levi smirked. "Oh, really? We'll see about that. I've got a plan for my fort this year that will knock their socks off."

His parents laughed and he wished them a goodnight before heading toward the house. He reached for his phone a time or two, wanting to send Rachel a text, but decided against it. He would let her have a peaceful night's sleep, and hopefully she wouldn't be too disappointed when she found out about her cancelled flight in the morning. Maybe she would even be a little bit happy about it. He hoped so.

In spite of the full day he'd had, Levi tossed and turned during the night, anxious to see Rachel again. He woke even earlier than his usual predawn hours to get a head start on his chores. The snow continued to fall, and even in four-wheel drive, he almost got stuck twice on his way to feed the cattle. Once that task was finished, he headed back, cresting the rise in the hill where he got cell service again, and a text came through from Rachel.

I just heard that the airport's closed. It looks like I'll get to watch some of your Christmas traditions after all.

His heart did a little flip as he stopped the truck to reply. *I'm sorry about your flight, but I am excited to spend Christmas with you.* Maybe that was too forward, but he didn't care. It was how he felt. *Have you told your mom yet? Is she going to be okay?*

Yes. I called her right after I found out and she's disappointed but she understands. She's planning to spend the day with my Aunt Julie and her family. I think my friend Sage is more upset than my mom. I always come to her Christmas Eve party. But she'll have plenty of other friends to keep her company.

Good. I'm sure she understands too. There's nothing you can do about the snow, so it's out of your hands. He paused, half-tempted to ask if there was anyone else who would be disappointed ... namely, Mark. But he didn't want to be nosy.

What time will you be back? Garrett said you're out feeding the livestock. I wish I could have come to watch or even help you. Will you be back in time for the fort competition? Your brothers are drawing up plans for theirs.

He smiled, warmed by the fact that she wished she could be with him. *You can come help me feed the cattle tomorrow morning, if you like. But I don't expect you to get up that early if you're not up for it. I'll be home soon. Want to be on my fort-building team?*

I don't know ... that would mean we would have to work together instead of competing against each other. ;) I was kind of looking forward to beating you again.

He laughed out loud, shaking his head as he replied. *You may have beaten me in pool, but I have a feeling you're a little less experienced when it comes to snow. You don't have to take me up on the offer, but it stands if you want it.*

I'm willing to join forces with you ... just this once.

You'll thank me later.

We'll see.

He set the phone aside and started driving again, frustrated that the snow kept him from going faster but at the same time grateful for the storm. It meant more time with Rachel, and this year, that was all he wanted this Christmas.

CHAPTER 13

*R*achel's arms ached from spending the morning helping Levi construct a massive snow fort, but it was worth it. She'd taken pictures of the forts and contestants before stowing her camera away and Levi gave the all clear for everyone to let the snowballs fly. Her sides ached from laughing as they'd dodged snowball attacks and taken aim at the others involved in the competition. He'd been right, she didn't know much about working with the snow, and he'd given her tips on how to make the fort secure. But she'd been the pitcher on her high school softball team, so when it came to throwing snowballs, she was definitely holding her own.

"Watch out!" Peter yelled, ducking for cover. "Rachel's throwing another one!"

She laughed and aimed the snowball at Garrett, winding back and letting it fly. It hit him right in the center of his back, leaving a white mark. He yelled and dove for the protection of his fort.

"Yes!" Levi cheered, giving her a high five as they laughed and dropped back into their fort.

"Oh," Rachel sighed, holding her stomach as the laughter died down. "I can't remember the last time I've had this much fun."

"Me either." Levi grinned, his eyes dancing with admiration. "I had no idea you used to be a pitcher. Good thing I asked you to be on my team."

"With your fort building skills and my aim, we're killing it," she said, turning to give him a smirk. "Maybe joining forces wasn't such a bad idea after all."

"I'm not hating it." The teasing look in his eyes turned to something deeper ... something that warmed her all the way down to her snow boots.

Rachel's heartbeat quickened. If Levi wasn't careful, he would melt the fort around them with the heat of his gaze. Her mouth went dry, but she couldn't look away. "What's our next move?" she asked, reaching for another snowball.

Levi caught her gloved hand in his, keeping hold of her gaze. "I've got one in mind ... but it doesn't have to do with snow."

Her breath caught as he gave her a half-smile, his eyes dropping to her lips and back, silently asking her for permission.

She bit the inside of her cheek, knowing she shouldn't give in, but unable to resist anymore. They were hidden in the fort. What would one little kiss hurt? She leaned forward, her heart hammering in aching expectation as Levi leaned toward her, the musky scent of his cologne throwing her senses into overdrive as their lips met, causing an explosion of fireworks in Rachel's chest.

Levi's kiss was soft, tentative at first. He put his hand behind her head, drawing her closer as his mouth moved with hers, bathing her in a shower of warm sparks. The kiss deepened, and Rachel sighed, unable to get enough of him as the rest of the world faded around them. She'd been kissed before, but never like this. Never in a way that made her feel as if her whole body was being consumed by delicious fire. Levi kissed a trail along her jawline, making her toes curl before he moved back to her mouth.

"Caught you!" Tommy yelled as he stuck his face into the fort.

Rachel and Levi instantly pulled apart as Tommy threw a snowball at Levi's head close-range.

It hit Levi in the side of the forehead and he brushed it off. "You little rascal," he said, slightly breathless as he reached for a snowball. "You're gonna pay for that."

Tommy shrieked and disappeared from view. Rachel laughed and brushed the snow from Levi's dark hair.

He gave her a wry smile. "Seriously, his timing couldn't have been worse." His eyes still smoldered, inviting her back.

She ached to pick up where they'd left off, but she hesitated. "Do you think Tommy saw us?" she asked, biting the edge of her lip.

Levi shrugged. "Even if he did, he's too focused on the battle to say anything. Especially after I get him with this." He grinned and stood, launching the snowball.

Rachel peeked out of the fort in time to see Tommy yell and shake the snow off of his beanie as he kept running toward his own small fort.

She laughed. "You have pretty good aim, yourself."

"You aren't the only one who's played some ball," he teased.

A snowball hit the side of their fort and Rachel squeaked, dropping for cover again. "They're getting more aggressive, what's our game plan?" she asked in an attempt at distraction.

"I kind of like the game plan we had going on," he said with a cajoling smile.

She pressed her lips together, longing to give in, but she shook her head. "We shouldn't. I want to … but we shouldn't."

He sighed and leaned back against the wall of the cave. "I guess you're right." He took her gloved hand and kissed it, his brown eyes holding hers. "But you should know that this is by far my favorite snow cave competition I've ever been in."

She laughed. "Mine too."

He studied her. "If you're worried about Tommy saying anything to my parents about the kiss, don't be. They adore you and would be thrilled if you and I started dating." He rubbed the back of his neck and he cleared his throat. "I mean—if that was what you wanted." He paused, searching her expression.

Rachel sucked in a breath in an attempt to steady her racing heart. "I'm open to the idea," she said with a coy smile. That was an understatement. She was definitely more than open to the idea of dating Levi.

His mouth curved up in one corner. "I'm glad to hear that."

She had to look away from him or she would be right back in his arms, and as much as she wanted that, she couldn't get ahead of herself. "I just ... " she continued, frowning slightly as she picked up a snowball, absent-mindedly moving it from hand to hand. "I think it's better if we wait until I'm not working here. What about your policy on not dating guests?" She glanced up at him.

"It's not an actual policy ... more of a personal rule." The corner of his lip curved up. "And I'm willing to make an exception in your case." He held her with a steady gaze.

Rachel swallowed. This would be so much easier if he wasn't insanely attractive. Her heart pumped loudly in her ears. "I can't ask you to do that, Levi," she said. Even though she wanted to. Badly.

"You don't have to. It's my choice." He shook his head. "I don't care how it might look. I don't care if it's not entirely professional." He reached for her other hand so that he held both of her hands in his. "I have feelings for you, Rachel. And I want to see where things might lead between us."

Her pulse stuttered and she squeezed his hands. "I want that too. Just ... not quite yet." His expression fell and she hurried on, "As soon as I get home though." She tilted her head, trying to coax a smile from him. "It's only a few days. We can wait that long."

"Speak for yourself," he teased.

She balked, pretending to be offended. "What? Are you saying I'm not worth the wait?" Without thinking she lightly tossed the snowball at him, hitting him in the chest. His eyes widened and she realized too late her mistake.

"Oh, it's on," he said, grinning as he grabbed a snowball.

Rachel squealed and ran from the fort, dodging snowballs and laughing as she ran in a zigzag pattern away from Levi, heading behind the barn for cover. A snowball hit the side of the barn and she heard Levi's disappointed groan. She laughed but didn't stop, turning toward the side of the barn away from the onslaught of the snow fort battle.

"Oh no you don't," Levi said.

She squealed as he caught her, tackling her into the fresh powder, using his body as a cushion as he held her tight before he rolled her onto her back, gently pinning her hands beside her head as he leaned over her.

"You think you can just chuck a snowball at me and not have any consequences?" he teased, his eyes brimming with laughter.

Rachel was breathless from her sprint but she smirked up at him. "I'm not scared of you, Levi Davis."

"Oh yeah?" He grinned wickedly and arched an eyebrow, his gaze deepening as he brushed a strand of hair from her face.

Rachel swallowed. Okay, maybe she was scared—scared of how little control she had on her heart. She couldn't take it anymore. She reached her hand behind his neck and pulled him to her.

His kiss was achingly soft, as if he was afraid he might break this fragile new thing between them. She pulled him closer and his kiss intensified, hungry and demanding. She was heedless of the snow at her back, all she could think about was Levi. She ran her hands through his hair and he sighed against her lips, bathing her in warmth before he reluctantly pulled back, cupping a hand to the side of her face, his eyes smoldering and still somehow tender. "To answer your question—you *are* worth the wait. I'll wait as long as you need, Rachel."

She stared, unable to breathe at the intensity of his gaze. Her heart swelled with the things she wanted to say, but she would save it for a time when she could say them in his arms. "Thank you," she said, giving him a faint smile.

He nodded, studying her face for another second before he stood and offered his hand to help her up. They dusted the snow off of their snow clothes and started heading back toward the forts.

Levi stooped and picked up a handful of snow, compacting it into a snowball. "We'd better prepare some ammo if we want to make it back to our fort. I'll cover you while you run."

Rachel laughed and shook her head as she scooped up a snowball of her own. "I seem to remember you missing your aim a few minutes ago. How about *I* cover *you* while you run?"

He chuckled. "That's probably a better idea." He gave her a wistful look. "Let me know when you're ready, okay?"

He was talking about running toward the fort, but his expression said there was another meaning to his words as well. She pressed her lips together and nodded. "I will."

CHAPTER 14

*L*evi had never had a more enjoyable Christmas Eve. All of the guests had taken the news of being snowed in better than expected. Several that had joined in the snow fort competition were now involved in the gingerbread house competition in the dining hall.

Levi and Rachel had helped to set up and then entered the competition themselves, working side by side at one of the long tables. Rachel was piping icing onto the roof of her gingerbread house, chatting with Paisley who'd come to join in the activities now that Hannah was feeling better. She laughed at something Paisley said and Levi's stomach gave a little flip. He adored the sound of her laugh and the way her blue eyes sparkled with her smile. Unable to help himself, he pulled out his phone and took a picture of Rachel and his sister, catching them by surprise.

Rachel arched an eyebrow at him. "Are you sneaking pictures?" she asked in a playfully accusatory tone.

He shrugged. "I figured I'd take a page from your book and snap a few candids."

Her lip twitched. "You're trying your hand at photography now?"

"Maybe." He smiled, knowing she'd called his bluff.

Paisley looked between them with an amused expression. "I'm glad Hannah's feeling better so I could see this."

Levi turned to her. "See what?"

"This." She gestured a circle around them, her hands slightly dotted with frosting. "You guys are cute."

Levi's eyes flicked to Rachel and she blushed. He looked back at his twin sister, unsure how to respond. "Um," he stammered, relieved when Paisley's husband Jake chose that moment to join them carrying Hannah on his hip. "Hi, Jake. Hey there, Hannah," Levi greeted without hesitation. He held his hands out to his niece. "Want to come see Uncle Levi?"

Hannah reached for him and his heart melted as she cuddled against his chest. "I've missed you, baby girl. Did you miss me?" he asked. At not quite one-year old, Hannah only said a few words, but she gave him a big smile and put her chubby hands on both sides of his face.

"Oh my goodness, she is adorable," Rachel said, stepping over to touch Hannah's shoulder. "Hi, sweetheart. I'm so glad you're feeling better."

"We're glad too," Paisley said. "I always get so stressed out when she's sick. Even though Christmas doesn't really mean anything to her yet, I would have felt bad if she was sick over the holidays."

"We need her with us on Christmas morning," Levi agreed. "I can't wait for her to open the present I got her." He turned to his brother-in-law, realizing he hadn't made introductions yet. "Jake, have you met Rachel?" he asked, nodding toward her. "She's the photographer my parents hired."

Jake stepped forward and shook her hand. "Hi Rachel. It's nice to meet you."

"It's nice to meet you, too." Rachel returned the handshake but her smile faltered into an apologetic frown. "Oops … sorry, I think I had frosting on my hands and might have gotten a little bit on you." She pointed at the cuff of his sleeve.

"No worries." He twisted to look at his sleeve. "With Hannah around, I usually have all kinds of stuff on my shirt." He winked and grabbed a nearby napkin, turning to Paisley. "Hannah just woke up from her nap so I thought I'd bring her over for a bit."

"I'm glad." Paisley nodded. "She's always happy after her naps. Look at those smiles she's giving Levi."

Levi had been so distracted by Rachel that he hadn't noticed Hannah beaming up at him. He smiled back at her, pressing his forehead to hers.

"She is such a cutie," Rachel gushed, turning to Paisley. "You know what? This might be the perfect time to get her pictures if you'd still like me to."

Paisley's face lit up. "I would love it! But no rush. I don't want to take you away from your gingerbread house." She nodded toward Rachel's detailed gingerbread chalet. "You should take first place for that."

"Oh, that's sweet of you," Rachel said. "But did you see the replica of Canyon Creek Ranch that one of the guests is making over there?" She gestured over her shoulder. "*That* is in a league all by itself."

Levi nodded and put a hand to the side of his face. "I think that woman came here just to show us all up," he stage-whispered.

Paisley laughed. "Yes. She really wanted that twenty-five-dollar gift card," she said dryly.

Rachel giggled and placed a final gumdrop on the path leading to her chalet before she stood back with a nod. "There. I'm all done. Let me go wash up and I'll be ready to take those pictures. We have to take advantage of these precious smiles." She touched Hannah's leg and then hurried off toward the kitchen.

Paisley and Jake turned to Levi as soon as Rachel was out of earshot. "Um—" Paisley said, pressing her lips together to hide and excited smile. "Can I just tell you how much I love her?" She jabbed a finger into Levi's arm. "Whatever you do, don't mess this up."

"Hey," he protested with a smirk, swatting her finger away. "What makes you think there's anything going on for me to mess up?"

Jake snorted and Paisley rolled her eyes. "Please. It's completely obvious. And I meant what I said before. You guys are cute." She grinned and tipped her head to the side. "Have you kissed her yet?"

"*Pais*," Levi moaned, keeping his focus on Hannah as he felt the telltale heat crawling up his neck.

Paisley gave a small squeal and covered her mouth with her hands. "Are you kidding me?" She smacked his arm, and he gave her a withering look.

"You know, it's not fair for you to stand there and attack me while I'm holding an infant," he chided.

She stepped closer, her brown eyes dancing with delight. "You *kissed* her?" She shook her head. "This is so fantastic. Have you planned when you're going to visit her in Arizona yet? Or even better, when she can come back out here?"

He squinted. "Not yet. This is all still new and we're waiting until she's done working here before we really define anything, so keep it under wraps for now, okay?"

She nodded and zipped her lip. "I won't say anything. But I don't know why you're waiting. Mom and Dad don't care if you date her ... is that what you guys are worried about?"

Levi shook his head, wishing he had a more satisfying answer. "I told her that, but she still thinks it would be best, so I'm trying to respect her wishes."

Jake grunted in affirmation.

Paisley shifted and her forehead creased as she folded her arms. "Could there be another reason though?"

Levi's stomach twisted. He didn't want to think about the hastily declined phone calls ... but there was still the mystery of Mark. "I don't know," he finally admitted.

"I'm sure she just wants to be professional," Jake said, nudging Paisley in the side. "Rachel's been hired to work here and she probably doesn't want to give the wrong impression to her employers. It's a good sign that she wants to wait." He gave Levi a reassuring nod.

"I guess so." Paisley didn't look convinced. "It will just be so much harder when it's long distance. It's too bad you can't use the time you have now to be together."

Levi agreed, but he couldn't say anything else because Rachel was approaching from the kitchen.

"Sorry that took me a minute," she apologized. "I was just helping your mom refill some candy bowls." She smiled at Hannah in Levi's arms. "What do you say, Miss Hannah? Should we do a photo shoot?" Hannah reached for Rachel, and Rachel's eyes widened in delight. "I'll take that as a yes," she said, looking at Levi for permission.

"Here you go." He passed Hannah to Rachel, his heart climbing to his throat at the way his niece cuddled right into her. Rachel looked good holding a little one. She would look good doing anything. Man, he was falling hard. Too hard. The truth was he didn't really know where she stood. What if she was only saying she wanted to wait until she got home as an excuse because it would be easier to tell him she wasn't interested? What if he was misreading all the signals again?

While Rachel and Paisley discussed where to take Hannah's pictures, Levi ran a hand through his hair, an idea forming. He waited for a pause in their conversation before clearing his throat. "I'd love to come watch, but one of the horses was a bit lame yesterday and I'd better go check on him."

"Not Cal, I hope?" Rachel frowned in concern.

He shook his head. "This is an older horse named Chester. We probably should have sold him a while ago, but he's one of my dad's favorites and he can't seem to part with him."

Rachel smiled and tilted her head. "How sweet."

"Tell Chester hello from me," Paisley said.

"If you need help hitching the team for the sleigh ride tonight, I'm happy to help," Jake added.

"Thanks, man." Levi waved at the group, his eyes holding Rachel's momentarily. She gave him a warm look that got his heart pumping before he turned and walked away. Maybe he was taking a risk with Rachel, and maybe he was a fool for falling so hard when he wasn't completely sure if she returned his feelings. But one thing was for sure—it was too late now. She'd captured his heart and there was no turning back.

CHAPTER 15

*R*achel adored doing baby photoshoots, and Hannah made it easy. She was quick to smile and by the time they were done with the shoot, Paisley was so grateful she looked close to tears. Rachel assured her it had been her pleasure and promised to get the finished file to her soon.

"Will you be joining us for caroling and the midnight sleigh ride?" Paisley asked as they left the lodge library where they'd taken pictures of Hannah on a sheepskin rug.

"I plan to, if that's alright?" Rachel said.

Paisley nodded, carrying Hannah on her hip. "Of course! I hope Levi told you our policy at the ranch—the more the merrier, always."

She smiled. "He did. And I love how welcoming your family is. It's really unique."

"It is?" Paisley seemed surprised.

Rachel laughed. "Yes. I guess maybe you're used to it since you grew up here, but back in the city, finding people so warm and hospitable is rarer than you'd think."

"Huh." Paisley shifted Hannah to her other hip and smiled. "Well thanks for the compliment. It's definitely a great place to be and there's nowhere else I'd rather live." She gave Rachel a side-eye. "Do you think you might come back to visit sometime?"

Rachel blushed. "I hope so. To be honest, I wasn't too disappointed about being snowed in. Thinking about leaving makes me sad."

"Because of the ranch ... or because of the company?" She gave her a sly smile and Rachel laughed.

"Both," she admitted, unable to hold back her smile.

Paisley nodded. "I can think of someone who's going to miss you when you leave."

Rachel's heart fluttered. "Did he say anything to you?"

"He didn't have to. I know when my brother's smitten." Paisley tilted her head. "I hope it works out for you guys. I don't think I've ever seen Levi this happy."

Rachel bit her lip, her chest filling with warmth. "I feel the same way."

"Well in that case, I hope you're able to sneak in a kiss or two before you leave." She winked, laughing as Rachel's blush deepened. "But don't worry, I won't say anything to anyone ... not that they don't already know," she teased. "My parents would be thrilled about it, so don't feel like you have to pretend for their sakes."

"Thanks," Rachel smiled faintly and left it at that. She wanted to take Paisley's word for it. She ached to run to Levi that second and throw her arms around him for another kiss, but the professional in her wouldn't allow it. Just a few days, or however long the storm lasted, and she would be free to pursue her feelings. Plus, she'd run headlong into a relationship with Mark and she didn't want to make that mistake again.

She couldn't believe he'd called last night. He had the worst timing, and she was annoyed he kept trying to reach her even after she was clearly ignoring his calls. Hopefully he would take the hint and move on.

They entered the lobby and Paisley took in a deep breath. "It smells like dinner is starting. Every Christmas Eve, my mom makes the best prime rib you've ever tasted. I'd better see if she needs any help."

"I'll come too. I'm happy to help."

Paisley shook her head. "That's sweet, but I already know my Aunt Beverly will be helping, and you know what they say about too many cooks in the kitchen." She winked. "Go relax for a bit and I'll see you at dinner."

Rachel hesitated. "Okay … if you're sure?"

Paisley nodded and held up Hannah's hand to wave. "Bye bye."

She grinned at Hannah and returned the wave. "Bye, cutie pie." After Paisley and Hannah left, she put her hands on her hips, debating what to do next. The mood in the lodge was lively and festive, and her first impulse was to find Levi, but if he was busy helping the injured horse, she didn't want to interrupt him. She'd taken enough pictures of the lodge, cabins and surroundings to fill three websites with, though she kept her camera around her neck just in case.

Her gaze wandered to the large fir tree with wrapped gifts beneath. Tomorrow was Christmas morning and the family would exchange their presents. The thought of Levi opening his gifts made her smile, and a sudden idea struck. As if on cue to help her, Garrett came striding around the corner and she waved at him. "You're just the person I'm looking for."

He raised both eyebrows and pointed at his chest. "Me? Are you sure you don't have me confused with someone else? An older brother perhaps?" He gave her a crooked smile and she laughed.

"Well, it might have something to do with him."

He dropped his shoulders in pretend disappointment. "It figures."

"I had a question for you. Do you guys own a colored printer, by chance?"

He nodded. "We have a nice one and you're welcome to it. What do you need it for?"

She pressed her hands together, delighted that her plan might work. "I'll tell you, but you have to promise to keep it a secret, okay?"

"You're in luck. I'm a pro at keeping secrets." He zipped his lip. "Follow me and I'll show you where the printer is. We keep it in the main office."

"Thanks." She smiled, giddy with anticipation as she followed Garrett.

He glanced at her over his shoulder. "Are you sure you don't have a younger sister?" he teased. "Because that would absolutely make my day."

She laughed. "None that I'm aware of," she paused, wrinkling her brow in thought. "I do have a cute best friend, but she's dating someone." It was too bad, too, because Rachel had a feeling that Sage and Garrett would have gotten along really well.

"Well that's not helpful," he said dryly. "Unless *she* has a sister?"

Rachel laughed again. "Sadly, no. But if I hear of any cute, single ladies, *or* their sisters, I'll be sure to recommend that they come visit the ranch," she said before realizing that was the last thing she would do while Levi worked here. A cowboy that handsome would be a prime target for female attention and she was suddenly grateful for his "keeping things professional with the guests" rule.

"Thanks. I'd appreciate that," Garrett said with a grin. "I'm beginning to think the only way I'll meet someone is if she's a guest."

"There aren't any girls you're interested in in Clearwater?"

He shook his head. "I've already dated the girls my age there. It's a small town, so the dating pool wasn't much to speak of. Not like Phoenix." He smiled.

"It can be hard to find someone to date, even in a big city," she countered. "The population may be bigger, but finding a *decent* guy is the tricky part."

"That's too bad. But I can tell you right now, Levi's a decent guy." Garrett shrugged, giving her a sideways look. "Too decent, if you ask me. I hope he's letting his guard down once in a while." He winked.

Rachel's cheeks heated as she fumbled to come up with an answer. "He's a great guy," she finally managed.

"He is." He shook his head as he led her into the office. "And he's one lucky son-of-a-gun."

She smiled, pretending not to understand his meaning as she asked questions about the printer and made her game plan. If she was quick about it, she could finish her scheme and still be done in plenty of time for dinner. She missed Levi and couldn't wait to see him again. As if in answer to her thoughts, her phone dinged with a text and she checked the screen, her heart tripping when she saw it was from Levi.

I'm looking forward to spending time with you tonight. I'll save you a seat at dinner.

She beamed and typed a quick reply.

I can't wait.

Dinner was a joyous occasion with the dining hall filled with the sounds of excited chatter and laughter. The Davis family and ranch guests were ringing in the holidays with the best meal Rachel could remember. Paisley hadn't been kidding about the steak, and the festive sides, desserts, and holiday punch were too good to pass up. Levi kept his leg pressed against hers during the meal, and from time to time he would reach down and rest his hand on her knee beneath the table-cloth. Every time he touched her, her body reacted with a warm, buzzing current of sparks. Between the amazing food and his subtle flirting, she never wanted the evening to end, but eventually the crowd moved from the dining hall to the great room where they sang carols at the piano.

Again, Levi stood next to Rachel, his fingers brushing against hers whenever he could manage it, and she loved the sound of his deep baritone as they sang along with the familiar holiday favorites. As the hour got later, the carols wound down and the guests left to their rooms with happy smiles on their faces, some of them promising to meet in the barn for the midnight sleigh ride. When only the family remained, Tommy hopped up and down excitedly.

"Do we get to open our present now?" he asked.

Claire nodded. "Let's go on over to the house and do our gift exchange, and then we'll get ready for the sleigh ride."

Peter and Alex's faces brightened as they and the rest of the family made their way out of the great room. Rachel stayed where she was, unsure if she should follow.

Levi sensed her hesitation. "Is everything okay?" he asked.

"Yes, it's great." She shifted. "I'm just thinking maybe I'll head to my cabin and meet up with you guys later for the ride. I don't want to impose on your family time."

He shook his head, his face determined. "Not on your life. You're part of our family tonight." He pressed his hand to the small of her back to steer her toward the group.

"You're sure I won't be in the way?"

"Positive." He gave her a reassuring nod. "The gift exchange is fun; you won't want to miss it."

"Okay … thanks." In truth, she'd always wondered what it would be like to watch a big family opening presents. With just her and her mom, most Christmas mornings were over fairly quickly. She allowed him to guide her toward the retreating group, disappointed when he finally dropped his hand from her lower back. Why had she insisted on keeping things professional? It would be so nice to hold Levi's hand right now, or to lean her head on his shoulder as she watched the family open presents. *Ugh.* It was torture keeping her distance, but she could hold strong. She could.

Hope and Owen were in the back of the group, and Rachel was grateful for the distraction when Hope asked how she'd liked the yoga session that morning. Rachel couldn't say enough about how much she'd loved it and even asked Hope if they could take a selfie together that she could send to Sage. Hope readily agreed, and Owen offered to take the picture for them. Rachel felt Levi's gaze on her as she and Hope smiled for the camera, her eyes meeting his after it was taken. Her breath caught at the warm look he gave her. If Hope and Owen hadn't been standing there, she would have caved and thrown herself into his arms.

"I'm touched that your friend is such an avid fan," Hope said, breaking her from her thoughts. "Why don't I give you my phone number and she can call me sometime if she wants. I'd love to chat with her and get her take on which episodes are her favorites."

"Really?" Rachel's eyes popped. "Oh my goodness, Sage is going to flip. That's so nice of you."

Hope smiled. "I'm looking forward to hearing from her." She gave Rachel her number and then pointed at her phone. "You almost have the same color of phone case as I do." She held up her aqua case.

Rachel laughed. "We're phone twins. We must have similar tastes."

Owen tipped his head. "You even almost look like sisters," he commented as he put an arm around Hope. "Both of you with blonde hair and blue eyes, and both of you somehow tan in December." He winked and kissed Hope's temple. "Although that's not surprising with how much time Hope spends outside."

"That's Texas in the winter for you." Hope smiled. "I love that it's mild year-round. The snow is fun for the holidays, but I don't know how you can handle it for the rest of the year, Levi."

He shrugged. "I don't mind it."

"I think it's gorgeous," Rachel agreed. "And it would be so nice to have the change in seasons. I like Arizona, but I could definitely get used to this." She gestured to the falling snow as they made their way outside. She realized a moment too late she'd forgotten her coat. As if reading her mind, Levi shrugged out of his coat and handed it to her.

"I don't need it," he said. "Go ahead."

"Thanks." She smiled at him, her heart skipping a beat as he helped her into the sleeves.

Hope and Owen hadn't noticed they'd stopped and kept walking toward the house. Soon Rachel and Levi were walking alone in the peaceful night.

Levi reached for her hand. "Is this alright?" he asked, searching her eyes.

She nodded, his touch sending warmth through every part of her as they slowed their pace. "Tonight has been perfect," she said softly, not wanting to disrupt the stillness with words.

"I've never had a better Christmas Eve." He gave her a crooked smile. "Would it be wrong to admit that I'm glad the airport closed?"

Her heart leaped into her throat. "Would it be wrong to admit I wish it would keep snowing so I wouldn't ever have to leave?"

He stopped walking and traced the back of his hand lightly down her cheek. "I don't want you to go either. The only thing that makes it easier is that I'll be free to date you when you're not working here anymore." His forehead creased. "But I'm missing you already, Rachel." He lifted her hand and pressed a kiss to her knuckles.

Rachel's mouth went dry. "I know. I missed you while we were apart this afternoon," she confessed. "It's going to be so much harder when we're in completely different states."

He nodded. "I've been thinking about that too. It's an obstacle, but it's one I'm willing to work around if you are?"

She swallowed, warmth spreading through her at the earnest look in his deep brown eyes. "Definitely." They stared at each other for a long moment and her breathing slowed, her gaze dropping to his lips. "It's nice to have a minute alone with you," she said softly.

"We'd better not let it go to waste." His gaze deepened as he pulled her over to stand beneath the roof of the barn and wrapped her in his arms.

Rachel hugged him back, relishing the warmth of his embrace as the snow fell silently around them. It was like their own private sanctuary, and she wanted to remember the moment forever. She tipped her face back and Levi didn't hesitate, pressing his lips to hers with a hunger that stole her breath away. She returned his fervor and they kissed for a few minutes before she pulled back, her heart pounding so hard it threatened to beat right out of her chest. "We'd better join your family or they'll wonder what happened to us."

"I think they'll have a pretty good idea," he said, giving her a coy smile as he reluctantly let her go, taking hold of her hand. "But as much as I'd love to keep you all to myself, I don't want you to miss the gift exchange."

"Good point." She was touched that Levi wanted her to be a part of the family gathering even though she had nothing to exchange. They walked toward his house, stomping off their feet on the front porch before he opened the door. A wave of warmth hit Rachel as soon as she stepped inside, along with the smell of freshly baked cookies and the sound of happy conversation against the backdrop of Christmas music playing. Her throat tightened. She had no idea Christmas gatherings like this actually existed outside of cheerful made-for-TV movies. The longing to be a part of it rose up in her chest like an expanding balloon as Levi led her into the living room.

"There you two are," Claire said, hopping up from her place on the couch to usher them to some empty chairs that had been set up around the tree. "You're just in time. We're about to open presents."

"*One* present, Tommy," Peter reminded his younger brother.

Tommy rolled his eyes. "I know, I know."

"Levi, you look a little flushed," his cousin Cody teased. "You must have found a way to stay warm in the storm out there."

The room erupted with laughter and Rachel blushed, unable to hold back a guilty smile as Levi shook his head at his family. "I don't know what you guys are talking about," he said, holding the chair for Rachel before he took his seat. "Are we doing youngest to oldest this year, Mom?" he asked, changing the subject.

There were a few more hoots of laughter before the focus turned away from them and onto the gifts. Rachel watched delighted as Hannah was given the first gift.

Levi leaned over to whisper in her ear. "Sorry about that," he apologized. "And I told you my parents didn't care." He gave her an amused look that made her heart stutter.

She pulled her lip between her teeth. Apparently, everyone in his family knew about their attraction, and judging by the big smiles they were giving her, they didn't mind one bit. Levi raised an eyebrow, his gaze moving to her mouth before he glanced away with a small smile. Rachel's heart galloped. Maybe there wasn't any point in pretending anymore, but as much as she wanted to, she couldn't bring herself to reach for his hand with everyone watching. But if he reached for hers, she would take it.

She enjoyed the gift exchange, smiling each time someone opened their gift. Alex had just unwrapped a hilarious pair of onesie pajamas made to look like a reindeer. He tried them on and Rachel's sides hurt from laughing at the sight of the seventeen-year-old wearing antlers and a fuzzy tail on the back. He was a good sport and posed while she took a picture.

"I think it's Rachel's turn next," Levi said after the laughter died down.

She turned to him with a confused frown. "I'm not getting a gift. I'm just here to take pictures," she said, holding up the camera.

"You're not getting a gift?" he repeated, scratching his chin. "Huh. Well then I wonder who this is for?" He reached under his chair and pulled out a wrapped box, handing it to her.

She read her name on the tag and gaped at him. "You got me a gift?"

He shrugged, his mouth pulling up in one corner. "I think Santa might have dropped it off early."

She shook her head. "I can't believe this." The room was quiet as she unwrapped the box, opening the lid to reveal a set of red fleece pajamas with a pretty snowflake pattern. "I love them!" She held up the pajamas for everyone to see. "Thank you, Santa," she said, earning laughter in return before the attention moved to Garrett whose turn was next.

She hugged the pajamas against her chest and nudged Levi in the side. "Thank you," she said quietly. "That was so sweet of you."

His eyes held uncertainty. "Don't feel like you have to wear them if you don't like them. I had to guess on your size and I admit I'm not much of a fashion expert, but the saleslady seemed to think they'd be a good choice."

Her heart melted. "When did you have time to buy them?"

He shifted. "I may have fibbed a bit about Chester being lame. I needed an excuse to head into Clearwater when I knew you'd be busy taking Hannah's pictures."

"Levi." She shook her head, too touched to say anything else so she leaned over and gave him a hug, not caring that his family saw. "Thank you so much. It means the world that you made a special trip into town just for me."

"I couldn't let you spend Christmas without your traditions," he said, holding her tight before reluctantly letting her go.

"I just feel bad that I don't have anything for you." At least not yet.

He shook his head, his eyes meeting hers as he lowered his voice. "Spending Christmas with you is the only gift I want, Rachel."

Her heart turned to liquid in her chest and she blinked back moisture. She would have kissed him right then and there if Paisley hadn't spoken up.

"Sorry to interrupt you when it looks like you're in the middle of something," she said with a playful smile, "but you're up, big brother."

"I am?" Levi looked away from Rachel to face his sister. "You've already gone?"

She nodded and held up a pair of pajamas.

"A lot happens when you're off in lala land," his dad teased, winking at Rachel before handing Levi a gift bag.

She didn't mind the teasing anymore. In fact, she kind of loved it. The Davises made her feel like she fit right in, and all worry about keeping things professional with Levi melted away. She watched eagerly as he opened the bag, pulling out a solid long-sleeve navy pajama top and navy and gray plaid flannel pants. "Thanks, Mom," he said, turning to Claire.

"You're welcome, honey," she said.

The rest of the family opened their gifts and then cleaned up the ribbons and wrapping paper as hot cocoa and cookies were served.

Levi checked his watch. "I'd better go hitch up the sleigh now. Do you want to come with me?"

Rachel would love nothing better, but she had to be practical. "I need to go get my snow clothes on. Should I meet you back at the barn?"

"Yep. Take my coat so you stay warm. I would walk you there, but I don't want to make everyone wait for me to hitch up the team." He looked torn. "Want me to send Peter or Alex with you?"

She shook her head. She didn't want to burden anyone, and she'd walked the paths enough times to know where she was going. "I'll be fine. Do you want your coat back though?"

"You keep it. I'll stay warm hitching up the team."

She pursed her lips, about to argue but she could tell he wasn't going to budge on the issue. "Well thanks for letting me borrow it," she said. "I'll meet you by the barn in a little bit."

"Okay." He squeezed her hand, his eyes brimming with anticipation. "I'm excited. I think you're going to like this."

She smiled, tilting her face to look up at him. "Will you sit beside me?"

He nodded.

"Then I know I will."

He grinned and walked Rachel to the door, helping her into his coat again before they parted ways. She braced against the cold by tucking Levi's coat up to her chin and forged her way through the swirling snow, warmed at the thought that soon she would be on a sleighride with her favorite cowboy. She smiled to herself as she trudged toward her cabin. Maybe Christmas miracles existed after all.

CHAPTER 16

"*T*hanks for your help, boys," Levi said to Garrett and his cousins as they finished hitching up the team of Clydesdales to the sleigh outside of the barn.

"No problem." Garrett clapped him on the shoulder. "Enjoy the sleigh ride." He waggled his eyebrows. "I saved the back seat for you in case you wanted it."

Levi tipped his head in gratitude. "Thanks, man."

He shrugged. "I'm glad you've got someone. I'll be riding Dynamo so there's more room in the sleigh."

Levi did a quick count of the few guests wandering over. The sleigh could hold up to twenty people, and so far, it looked like they would be fine. The heavy snowfall from earlier might have deterred some of them … though it was letting up now, with only a few flakes drifting down. "Rachel and I can ride Cal if we need to." He didn't care if they were riding in the sleigh or double on horseback. As long as he was with her, he'd be happy.

"I think you'll be fine in the sleigh," Garrett said. "I'm gonna go saddle Dynamo."

"Sounds good." Levi checked the harness one more time, making sure it was secure.

"How's it looking, cowboy?"

His heart caught at the sound of Rachel's voice. He straightened, turning to face her. "Looks like we're all set." She wore her ever-present camera around her neck, and he took in her snow clothes with a nod of approval. "I'm glad to see you're all geared up. We typically go for about an hour and it can get cold."

"Speaking of which." She handed him his coat. "You'll probably want this. Thanks so much for letting me borrow it."

"Anytime." He shrugged it on as guests and family members congregated around the carriage.

His dad stepped into the driver's seat of the sleigh, calling everyone's attention. "Thanks for joining us for our traditional Christmas Eve sleigh ride," he said, smiling at the group. "Claire has some hot chocolate for anyone who would like some, and then if you'll find a seat in the sleigh, we'll head on out."

There was excited chatter as the guests migrated to Claire for hot chocolate. Levi turned to Rachel. "Would you like some?"

She rubbed her gloved hands together. "Yes, please. I already had a cup at your house, but it was so good, I can't resist having more."

He grinned. "One cup of cocoa, coming right up. Garrett saved the back seat of the sleigh for us if you want to get settled."

"Okay, that was nice of him."

He nodded. "He's been full of Christmas spirit lately."

"It's contagious around here." Her blue eyes glimmered as she held his gaze.

He wanted to lean down and kiss the faint smile on her lips, but hopefully there would be time for that later. "I'll be right back," he said, heading toward the group waiting for cocoa.

"I'll take a couple of pictures and then I'll hold our spot," she answered.

Levi got two cups of cocoa from his mom. "Enjoy the ride, sweetheart," she said with a wink.

He smiled. "You too." Everyone seemed to be winking at him lately, but he liked it. He liked the way his family had taken to Rachel and how they were so obviously hoping for something to happen between them. He was hoping for the same thing. She seemed to be less reluctant about showing affection in front of people after the gift exchange. He wasn't sure why, but he also wasn't about to question it. He would enjoy being with her tonight and not worry about when she might have to leave, though the lack of snowfall had him a little concerned.

The Kalispell airport was used to dealing with snow and could have the flights back up and running as soon as tomorrow if the storm was over. The sleigh ride would be more enjoyable without thickly falling snow in their faces, but if Levi could have his way, he would keep it falling for a week—even longer—if it meant having Rachel with him.

He walked to the back of the sleigh and handed Rachel the warm foam cup topped with a lid for sipping. "Here you go."

"Mm. Thank you." She cradled the cup in her hands. "I got some great pictures of the team and sleigh. Those horses are amazing. They look so strong and yet gentle at the same time."

"Elliot and Star are a great team," he agreed. "We pretty much only use them for sleigh and carriage rides, but they work together well."

"Star." She tipped her head to the side. "That's a nice, Christmassy sounding name."

He smiled. "It is. But Mom named her that because of the star mark on her forehead."

"Oh." She laughed self-consciously. "I have a lot to learn when it comes to horses."

"I'd be happy to teach you."

"I'd like that."

They locked onto each other's gaze and Levi's pulse kickstarted at the same time that the sleigh pulled forward. His cousin Owen had brought his guitar and started strumming familiar carols as everyone sang along.

Rachel reached for Levi's hand and he held it tight, his heart nearly filled to bursting. This was what he wanted; this, right here with Rachel. It was one of those moments so perfect it was almost painful. He glanced at her pretty profile as she smiled and sang along with the others. He never would have guessed that this desert-dwelling city girl would be the one to capture his heart and make him feel like his life was finally whole. But that's exactly what she'd done. He didn't know what the future would hold for them, whether she would come here or he would go to her in Arizona, but that didn't seem to matter anymore. All that mattered was that he would find a way to be together with her. She completed him.

As if sensing his thoughts, she turned, her voice trailing off from the song as she met his gaze. He simply stared at her, too moved to speak. He leaned toward her, gently brushing his lips against hers. She returned the kiss, tentative and sweet. His heart hammered and he pulled away, unsure how much public affection she was comfortable with. She gave him a warm smile and then leaned her head on his shoulder. He sighed and wrapped his arm around her, holding her close as the sound of the team's harness bells jingled merrily in the night.

Halfway through the ride, Levi's dad pulled the team to a stop. "We'll take a break here so you can enjoy the scenery and stretch your legs for a bit, and then we'll turn around and head back to the lodge," he announced.

Rachel lifted her head and let out a delighted gasp. "Is that a lake?"

Levi nodded. "That's Crescent Lake."

"Is it part of Canyon Creek property?"

"Yep. We come here to go swimming or fishing in the summertime. It's a nice spot to hang out."

"It's gorgeous with those mountains in the backdrop. And the sky has cleared enough to see some stars." Her face glowed with excitement. "I've got to get some pictures of this." Without waiting for him she hopped out of the sleigh and started framing her shots.

Levi chuckled and was about to follow her when he felt something hard in his coat pocket. He reached in and pulled out Rachel's phone. The screen flashed alive with the movement, showing a text message on the lock screen. His stomach turned to lead when he saw that it was from Mark.

Hey gorgeous, I'm missing you like crazy. When will you be home?

Bile rose in Levi's throat and he quickly pocketed the phone again, his heart thudding like a dull cannon in his ears. He glanced at Rachel as she stood taking pictures of the lake. She probably didn't realize she'd left her phone in his coat. He wouldn't say anything about seeing the text. He didn't want to ruin the evening with anger and accusations, but his blood ran cold. How could he have let his feelings get this involved? He thought he'd known her, but in reality she was a complete stranger, toying with his heart while all this time she had a boyfriend. Or worse—what if she was married? It was possible. Levi felt sick.

He climbed out of the sleigh and walked over to find Garrett who was chatting with Owen and Cody. He tapped him on the shoulder. "Hey, I need to borrow Dynamo."

Garrett turned, his brows pulling together. "What's wrong?"

Levi shook his head and held his stomach. "I'm not feeling well." It was true.

"Oh, dang. I'm sorry." Garrett gave him a sympathetic look. "What about Rachel?"

Levi glanced over his shoulder to where Rachel was still engrossed in taking pictures. "I'll let her know I'm taking off. You can have my seat and keep her company." He considered warning Garrett to keep his distance, but he knew his brother wouldn't flirt with Rachel now that he thought Levi was interested in her.

"Sure." Garrett frowned. "Do you need someone to ride back with you?"

"Yeah, Ava and I both rode on horseback and would be happy to go back with you," Cody offered.

"No. I'll be fine. Thanks." Levi waved at them and headed for Dynamo who stood waiting patiently a few feet away from the sleigh. He mounted and reluctantly steered the horse toward Rachel. She looked up at him from her camera lens, the big smile on her face changing to surprise.

"Are you going for a ride?" she asked, straightening as she lowered her camera.

He adjusted his seat in the saddle and cleared his throat, avoiding looking at her. "I'm afraid I've got to head back now. I'm not feeling very well."

Her forehead wrinkled in concern. "I'm so sorry. Is there anything I can do for you?"

You've already done enough. "No," he said flatly. "I just need to get back. Garrett will keep you company."

"Oh … okay," she said, her voice small and full of disappointment before she touched his leg. "I hope you get feeling better soon. I'd feel awful if you had to spend Christmas Day sick in bed."

"I'll be fine." He turned Dymano to leave.

"Levi," Rachel said, biting her lip. "Are you sure everything's okay?"

"Yep." His heart twisted. He wanted to confront her about Mark, but what good would it do? She would leave soon anyway and he would never see her again. He had to deal with this like a man. "Maybe I'll see you tomorrow."

"Okay. I hope so." She shifted. "Send me a text when you get back so I know you made it safe." She reached for her pockets, frowning in confusion before she snapped her fingers. "I think I might have left my phone in your coat. Do you mind checking?"

He felt for his pockets, pretending he didn't already know it was there before he reached in and handed the phone to her. "Good thing you remembered," he said, watching for her reaction to the text. To his frustration, she put it in her coat without checking the screen.

"Yes. Sorry I left it in there." She glanced up at him, her perfect features illuminated by the moonlight. "I don't want to keep you when you're not feeling well, but I have to tell you that this has been the best Christmas Eve I've ever had."

He swallowed, his heart splintering in two. "I'm glad you've enjoyed it," he said, his voice thick.

"I have." She smiled, dropping her hand from his leg. "Merry Christmas, Levi."

He winced inwardly. "Merry Christmas." He kept his expression passive as he turned Dynamo and lightly kicked his sides. The horse responded instantly, picking up into a trot, then a lope, then gallop.

He wasn't called Dynamo by accident, and Levi was grateful for his speed, urging the horse faster as they followed the packed trail left from the sleigh. If he could outrun the stabbing pain of his heart, he would keep on running and never stop.

CHAPTER 17

*R*achel woke early on Christmas morning, anxious to hear how Levi was feeling and not wanting to miss watching his family open presents in case he was feeling better. She grabbed her phone, her stomach dropping in disappointment when there was no text from Levi. Her mom had sent a cheerful text wishing her a Merry Christmas and Rachel typed a quick response, glad that there weren't any more messages from Mark. She'd blocked him after returning to her cabin late last night and reading his text. It was as if he'd completely forgotten that they'd broken up and ignored the fact that she hadn't returned his calls. Way too clingy. She'd felt relief as soon as she'd blocked him—but truthfully, she wouldn't mind a little more clinginess from Levi.

He'd acted so strangely last night. Maybe it was because he wasn't feeling well, but she couldn't shake the worry that there was more to it. She'd gone over their conversation on the sleigh ride but couldn't think of anything she might have said to chase him away like that. She hesitated for a moment and then sent him a text.

Merry Christmas! How are you feeling?

A knock sounded at the door and her heart did a somersault. She was wearing the red pajamas Levi had given her and had zero

133

makeup on, but she wasn't about to make him wait out on the porch. She hopped up from the bed and opened the door wide, her heart stinging with disappointment when she saw Peter standing there.

"Good morning, Rachel," he said, tipping his cowboy hat.

She smiled. "Good morning, Peter. Merry Christmas."

"Same to you." He put his hands at his waist. "How's your fire? Do you need me to stoke it for you?"

"Oh. Um …" She turned and looked over her shoulder at the dying coals. "Actually, that would be great, if you wouldn't mind."

"Nope."

She stepped aside and he removed his hat and came in, all business as he crouched by the fire and stacked fresh wood over the embers. "Have you opened your Christmas presents yet?" she asked.

"No, we're going to do that a little later. Now that the airport is open again, some of the guests are leaving this morning so we're going to wait until that settles down."

She blinked. "The airport is open?"

He turned. "Yeah. I figured Levi would have told you already."

She shook her head, her mind swirling as another disappointed stab hit her in the chest. Levi knew? Why hadn't he called her yet? And why had he sent Peter to help with her fire instead of coming himself? "Is he feeling better this morning?" she asked.

"Who?"

"Levi."

Peter shrugged. "Oh, I don't know. He seemed fine when he left to feed the cattle a little while ago."

She bit the inside of her cheek. If he was well enough to feed the livestock, he was probably fine. But why hadn't he invited her to come along with him to feed them? Something was definitely off.

"My mom is making calls to all of the guests about the airport, so I bet you'll be getting a call soon," he said, straightening from the fireplace where the logs were quickly catching fire. "I think this should do it for you. Can I get you anything else?"

"No. This is great. Thanks."

"Okay. Breakfast is going now until nine o'clock. My Aunt Beverly made her famous gingerbread waffles and they're really good."

She smiled weakly. "Thanks. I'll be over in a little bit." She didn't have much appetite so she wasn't sure she would be eating breakfast. She had to know what was going on with Levi. After Peter left, she checked her phone but Levi hadn't returned her text. *Don't jump to conclusions*, she chided herself. He probably didn't have service while he was feeding the cows. And maybe he didn't call to tell her about the airport situation because he wanted to let her sleep in after a late night ... or maybe he didn't want to tell her because he didn't want her to leave. The last thought warmed her, but it didn't jive with what she knew of him. He would tell her regardless; he wasn't selfish.

Her phone dinged and her heart leapt with hope, but it was only an email alerting her that the airport was open and her flight was scheduled to depart later that morning. The news sank like a lead ball in her stomach and her throat thickened. So much for her plans for spending Christmas with Levi. She'd been looking forward to spending the day with him, and now all of those plans were slipping away. In order to make her flight, she would have to start getting ready right now. What if she didn't even have time to say goodbye?

The cabin phone by her bed rang and she answered it. "Hello?"

"Hi Rachel, it's Claire. I'm sorry this is such short notice, but it sounds like the airport is open again. We're doing the first shuttle run in thirty minutes." She paused. "We were so excited to have you spend Christmas with us ... is there any chance you could postpone your flight?"

Rachel bit her lip. She'd wondered the same thing, but there was a fee to change the flight and the Davises had been generous enough paying for her airfare and letting her stay in the cabin for free. There was no way she'd put an extra charge on their card so she could extend her time. "That's so sweet of you. I was looking forward to spending Christmas here too, but I'd better get back."

"I understand." Claire's tone was heavy with disappointment. "Well, I hope I'll get a chance to give you a hug, but things are a bit crazy this morning. In case I don't see you, please know how much we've loved having you stay with us and we can't wait to see the pictures and videos you've taken. Don't take too long before you come back to visit, alright?"

"I won't. Thank you for hiring me for this job and for being such gracious hosts. I'll miss this place until I can come back again."

"We'll miss you too, honey." She sighed. "I wish I could chat longer, but I've got a few more phone calls to make. Take care, Rachel."

"You too. And Merry Christmas."

"Merry Christmas, and safe travels."

Rachel hung up the phone, disappointment searing through her as she rushed to get ready and pack so she could make the first shuttle. She tried not to think about the fact that Levi hadn't replied to her text yet. Would she not even have the chance to hug him goodbye? The Christmas of her dreams was slowly changing into a nightmare. She lugged her suitcase, backpack and camera case toward the lodge, cursing the traitorous blue sky that was the cause of her rapid change of plans. The shuttle was parked in front of the lodge with the engine running. Paisley walked forward to meet her with a sad smile.

"Good morning, Rachel. Sorry for all of this unexpected chaos." She reached for Rachel's suitcase and Rachel handed it over without protest.

"Thanks. And it's not your fault. *I'm* sorry we're interrupting your Christmas morning."

Paisley shrugged. "It just means that we get to draw the day out longer. We don't have any more guests coming in until tomorrow so we'll open presents later." She frowned. "I wish you could stay."

Rachel's heart twisted. "Me too." Maybe she should have just offered to pay the fee herself, but she would only be delaying the inevitable. "Have you seen Levi this morning? I can't seem to reach him."

"He's out feeding the cows," Paisley said, her face lined with sympathy. "He doesn't have cell service out in the fields. Did he not stop by your cabin this morning?"

Rachel shook her head, that sinking feeling that something was off settling back into her gut. "I haven't seen him since he left the sleigh ride last night."

Paisley raised both eyebrows. "He left? What do you mean?"

Rachel forgot that Paisley and Jake had opted out of the sleigh ride, not wanting to keep Hannah out in the cold when she'd just gotten over being sick. "We were at Crescent Lake and he said he wasn't feeling well, so he took Garrett's horse back. I haven't seen or heard from him since." He hadn't even texted her to let her know he'd made it back last night like she'd asked him to.

Paisley shifted. "Huh. That's really weird. I know he left to feed the cows this morning—although he does that even when he's sick. He's like my dad and gets his chores done no matter what. Once when we were sixteen, he went out to take care of them even though he had pneumonia. My mom had to chase him down and force him to go back home. He was running a fever and everything."

"Wow. That's dedication." Rachel's shoulders relaxed. Maybe that's all that was going on. Maybe Levi really wasn't feeling well and he hadn't checked in with her yet because he didn't know she was leaving. He would probably answer her text as soon as he could and she'd jumped to conclusions for nothing.

"I'm sorry you weren't able to say goodbye." Rachel squinted. "I wish we could wait until he comes back, but we'd better get going so everyone can make their flights," she said with an apologetic frown.

Rachel straightened her shoulders and nodded. "Of course. I don't want to hold anyone up." She forced a smile. "Besides, I hate goodbyes anyway." She nodded toward the guests piling into the van. "I'll go grab a seat."

"Okay." Paisley still looked sad but she turned her attention to helping the guests load their luggage.

Rachel took a seat toward the back of the van so that other passengers could take the front seats. She also needed a place to hide her feelings from Paisley. Emotion thickened in her throat as the van loaded up and they pulled away from Canyon Creek Ranch. She searched the road for any sign of Levi's truck, but the road was empty. She wanted to enjoy the scenery but her heart was too heavy. Now

137

that she wouldn't be spending Christmas Day with Levi, everything seemed dull and empty. She kept her phone in her hands, anxiously waiting for his text and half hoping he would chase her to the airport for a romantic kiss goodbye, but the drive to the airport passed without any word from him.

She masked her feelings as she gave Paisley a big hug. "Thanks so much for everything. I'm going to miss you," she said.

Paisley squeezed her back before pulling away to search her face. "You'll hear from him soon. Don't worry."

"Thanks." Rachel gave her a faint smile. "Will you give this to him … and tell him Merry Christmas for me?" She unzipped the front pocket of her suitcase and pulled out the gift she'd made for Levi, handing it to Paisley who accepted it with a mixture of surprise and sadness.

"You got him a present? That's so sweet." She shook her head. "I bet he had something for you, too. He'll probably send it later."

Rachel shrugged. "He already bought me pajamas, and I don't expect anything in return. It was just something I wanted to do."

Paisley smiled and gave her another hug. "Merry Christmas, Rachel."

"Merry Christmas." She swallowed back the lump in her throat, covering her emotion with a big smile. "Give Hannah a kiss for me."

"I will." Paisley waved.

Rachel waved back before heading into the terminal. She grimaced when she heard, "I'll Have a Blue Christmas," playing in the background. *Truer words were never spoken, Elvis,* she thought cynically. She'd never liked the song, and now without Levi to celebrate with, it would be a very blue Christmas indeed.

CHAPTER 18

*L*evi waited in his truck until he knew the shuttle was gone and he was safe to drive back. He'd gotten the information about the airport before leaving that morning and knew Rachel would be on the first shuttle to Kalispell. He was a coward, but the thought of facing her again was too much. He'd spent another restless night tossing and turning. At one point, he'd written a long text asking her who Mark was and demanding the truth, but then he'd deleted it and chucked his phone across his bed in frustration.

What was the point in calling her out on it? Either she would deny that she had a boyfriend or confirm it. If she confirmed it, hearing about it would twist like a knife in his gut, and if she denied it, he had no way of knowing whether or not she was telling the truth. She lived in Phoenix and had a completely separate life there. So unless he hired a private investigator—which he wasn't going to do—he would have to take her word for it. It was pointless to give the situation any more thought. Rachel was leaving and he would never see her again. The end.

Levi scrubbed a hand down his face and shifted his truck into drive, slowly pulling out of the field where he'd fed the cows and making his way back along the empty road. He flipped on the radio, but that stupid song about a blue Christmas was playing so he quickly switched it off again, clenching his jaw.

Normally when he was upset about something he worked hard until he could get it out of his system. But today was Christmas. The one day that they eased up on their regular chores and spent time together. Now that the airport was open, they wouldn't have more than a handful of guests that had booked over Christmas—and none of them were Rachel.

His heart stung and he pressed down on the accelerator, anxious to escape his own thoughts. He passed the rise on the road when he got cell service again and his phone chimed with texts. He slowed the truck to a stop to read the messages, his lungs squeezing when he saw that they were from Rachel.

Merry Christmas! How are you feeling?

He flinched, sensing her cheerfulness ebbing into worry as he read the next text.

The airport is back open and I have to leave soon. I hope I'll get a chance to say goodbye.

And finally.

Paisley said you're feeding cows and don't have service. I hope that means you're feeling better. I wish we had more time together. Please call me as soon as you get this. I miss you already.

He scoffed and set the phone down. *Sure she misses me,* he thought sarcastically. *She'll miss me until she's back home in Mark's arms.* He held the phone, debating what to do. He wasn't going to call her, but he didn't want to be a total jerk. He took a deep breath and typed a reply.

Sorry I missed you. I hope you have a good Christmas and a safe flight home.

Her answer came almost instantly.

Thanks! I'm just boarding my flight. I wish I didn't have to leave. I'm already looking at flights to see how soon I can manage to come back for a visit.

Levi lowered his phone and rested his forehead on the steering wheel. Why had he let his guard down? Why hadn't he stuck to his rules about not flirting with the guests? It felt like someone had reached into his chest and yanked his heart out ... and there was nothing he could do about it but let time heal the wound.

He hated himself for doing it, but he didn't respond to Rachel's text. He opened the glove box and pulled out the airline gift card he'd planned to surprise her with today. He'd imagined how fun it would be to watch her blue eyes light up with the surprise, and the excitement in planning how soon she could return. It was a selfish gift, really. One that he'd hoped would ensure that she would come back to him. He'd looked into roundtrip airfare to Phoenix but didn't want to assume too much. He'd planned to wait until she invited him there, and if she had, he would have taken the first available flight to see her.

He groaned and pressed his eyes closed, angry with himself for dwelling on what might have been. The bottom line was Rachel wasn't someone he could trust, and he couldn't be with someone like that.

He grabbed his phone and deleted the text thread before he could talk himself out of it, and then he tossed his phone onto the seat beside him and started driving again. It was better this way. She would move on with her life, and he would try to move on with his. Maybe he would throw himself into building his house on the property his parents had given him. It was past time to move out on his own.

On impulse, he turned off on an approaching side road rather than heading straight in the direction of the lodge. He didn't want to see his family right then and face their questions about Rachel. But more than that, he didn't want to go back to the lodge and miss her. Because he knew he wouldn't be able to help it. As much as he wanted to be angry about the situation, the ache in his chest told a different story. He wasn't angry. He was hurting. And the pain was so intense it nearly gutted him. He hadn't just liked Rachel; he'd fallen head over heels in love with her. And now he had to pay the price.

He pulled up to his property and cut the engine. The snow was too deep and he wouldn't be able to do anything until spring. He'd been excited to have a place of his own, but now even that seemed like an empty dream without Rachel as part of it. His phone rang, breaking through his thoughts. His heart pounded, wondering if she was calling before her flight took off. He checked the screen and exhaled, his shoulders slumping as he answered. "Hey, Garrett. What's up?"

"Where are you?" Garrett demanded. "Rachel had to leave on the first shuttle and you weren't here to say goodbye. Did the truck break down or something? Paisley said Rachel was really sad at the airport."

He winced. "I've been out feeding the cows."

"It doesn't take this long." He paused. "What's going on, Levi? First you leave the sleigh ride early, claiming to be sick, and now you don't even see her off? It's not like you to treat anyone like this, much less a girl you care about."

Levi took his cowboy hat off and raked a hand through his hair. "You're right," he admitted. "It's not like me. Something happened last night, but you have to swear not to say anything, okay? I don't want to taint anyone's views of Rachel."

Another pause. "What was it?"

He pulled in a breath, bracing himself against the pain. "She accidentally left her phone in my coat. There was a text message from someone named Mark. He's either her boyfriend or—someone special to her," he finished, not willing to contemplate the possibility she was married.

"How do you know that? Did you ask her about it?"

"I didn't want her to think I was prying, and I swear I wasn't. The text was right there on her home screen."

"You didn't even *talk* to her about it?" Garrett made a sound of disbelief. "Levi, I'm sure it was all a misunderstanding. Rachel doesn't seem like a cheater."

"I thought so too, but you should have seen this text. There's no way he's not her boyfriend." It pained him to speak the words out loud.

"What did it say?"

He sighed. "Something like, 'Hey gorgeous, I miss you like crazy and can't wait until you get home.'"

More silence on the other end. "Huh," he said in a deflated tone. "Yeah. It sounds like a boyfriend." He blew out a breath. "I'm sorry, man. I feel partly responsible. I was the one who brought her out here."

"It's not your fault. She could have told me that she was involved with someone else at any time, and she chose not to. That's on her."

"It still seems out of place with her character though."

Levi swallowed. He'd felt the same way, wanting to disbelieve the proof when it was right in front of him. He'd never felt such a strong connection in such a short amount of time with anyone as he had with Rachel—but the reality was he didn't know her. Not really. And that fact hurt almost more than anything else.

"Maybe she was thinking of breaking up with this guy, so she chose not to tell you about him?" he suggested.

"And that made kissing me okay?" Levi shook his head. "Even if she was planning to break up with him, that doesn't make it right."

"I know. I was just trying to give her the benefit of the doubt. And I still think you should talk to her. It would give you some closure."

"We'll see."

Garrett grunted. "Well, wherever you are, come home so we can start opening presents. Tommy and Peter are chomping at the bit."

"I'll head over. I just stopped by my property for a bit."

"See you soon."

"Bye." Levi ended the call and headed for home, trying not to think about the fact that Rachel was on her way home too … likely with a man named Mark waiting to pick her up from the airport.

CHAPTER 19

"*M*erry Christmas, sweetheart!"

Rachel accepted her mom's warm but brief hug at the pickup curb of the Phoenix airport. "Merry Christmas, Mom." Before she could say anything else, a car honked behind them and the driver pointed at the "No Waiting" sign.

Her mom waved at him. "I know, I know, we're going."

Rachel hurried to load her luggage and they pulled away from the pickup zone, heading into the congested city traffic.

"I'm surprised it's this crowded on Christmas," Rachel mused.

"It's always crowded," her mom returned with a shrug. "People don't know how to slow down these days—even on Christmas."

Rachel thought of Canyon Creek in contrast. The Davis family worked hard, but they also knew how to have fun and relax. There were still, peaceful moments, like at Crescent Lake or in the forest with Levi when she'd simply enjoyed the beauty around her.

"Tell me all about Montana," her mom continued. "I didn't want to bother you while you were working, but I can't wait to see your pictures."

Rachel turned her phone over in her hands, waiting for a reply from Levi. She was surprised he hadn't texted her back yet, but it was

Christmas. He was probably busy with family activities. The thought sent a sharp stab of longing through her, but at the same time made her happy. She hoped it was a special day for him and that he liked her gift. For now she would focus on having a nice Christmas with her mom.

She stretched her arms and smiled. "Montana was amazing. I did my research on Canyon Creek before I left, but nothing compared to seeing it in person." She sighed and shook her head in wonder. "It's gorgeous there, Mom. The scenery is so dramatic and stunning. I could have taken pictures there nonstop and still not even tapped the surface."

Shelby laughed. "I hope you at least took breaks to eat now and then."

"Oh yes, the food at the lodge was to die for."

"Sounds like I need to go visit." Her mom smiled. "Were the owners nice?"

"Claire and Joe are two of the nicest people I've ever met. They've got a big family and they all made me feel so welcome. You'll have to visit; I know you would love it. I plan to go back as soon as I can."

"Really?" Shelby turned to glance at her sideways, studying her before she looked back at the road. "Honey, you are positively glowing. If I didn't know any better, I would guess you met someone."

Rachel smiled and bit her lip. "Maybe—"

Her mom squealed. "What? Who is he? Someone at the ranch?"

She nodded. "The Davises oldest son, Levi. I got to know him really well and we just—" She paused, her smile growing as she struggled to find a word to adequately describe the chemistry between them. "—hit it off," she finished. It was a massive understatement, but she wasn't ready to confess she'd fallen in love after only a few days. She never would have thought it possible. But then again, she never expected to meet someone like Levi.

Shelby squealed again and squeezed her arm. "Tell me everything."

Rachel leaned back in her seat, still grinning like an idiot as she recounted everything to her mom, her heart doing little flips all over again as she relived the details.

"So when do I get to meet this incredible cowboy of yours?" Her mom asked as they pulled into the garage.

"I'm not sure. Hopefully soon." Rachel lifted a shoulder. "We talked about flying out to visit each other." She glanced at her phone again, fighting the disappointment that he still hadn't answered. From what she'd observed, Levi wasn't on his phone much, but she'd hoped he would be thinking of her … especially after Paisley gave him her gift. She pushed the worry aside and climbed out of the car to unload her luggage.

"It's too bad that he lives so far away," her mom said, helping to lift her suitcase from out of the trunk. "But based on how big your smile is, I'm sure you'll find a way to work things out. I'm happy for you, sweetie. I haven't seen you glow like this when you've talked about anyone—especially not Mark."

Rachel groaned and made a face. "Yeah. I totally had to block him."

Shelby raised her eyebrows. "What happened?"

"He kept calling me and then last night he left me this text saying that he missed me and couldn't wait for me to get home."

Her mom frowned. "I have to say I'm not too surprised. He was way too possessive. I was relieved when you broke up with him."

"I honestly don't know why I dated him in the first place. Hopefully he'll find someone who doesn't mind his clinginess, but I'm not that girl."

Shelby laughed. "No, you are not. You've always been a free spirit; not wanting anyone or anything to hold you back." She tipped her head to the side. "I'm guessing Levi isn't clingy then."

"Not at all." A little too much the opposite, in fact. Rachel refused to check her phone again. She'd taken it off of silent mode after her flight. If he called or texted, she would hear it. She forced a bright smile as they made their way into the house. "Have you opened your presents yet?"

"Of course not. What fun would it be to open presents by myself?" Her mom smiled. "Take your time settling in and then we'll open them together when you're ready."

"Sounds great. I won't be long." Rachel headed for her room and unpacked her suitcase, trying hard to ignore her phone, but with each minute that passed, the nagging feeling that something was off grew bigger. If Levi wasn't a big phone communicator, it was going to be challenging to try to have a long-distance relationship. She'd never thought of herself as needy, and she almost felt guilty for accusing Mark of being that way. But she'd thought Levi had been pretty clear about wanting to pursue something when she got home, and if he was feeling even half of what she was feeling, he would be anxious to talk to her.

She tossed her dirty clothes into a hamper, taking a moment to smile at the snowflake pajamas, before she left to join her mom and open presents. Maybe the Davises were still opening gifts. With a family that size, it probably took a long time. Maybe that's why Levi hadn't texted her yet. She pasted on a smile for her mom's sake, but deep down, the worry that he wasn't going to reply wouldn't leave her alone.

CHAPTER 20

"There you are. I've been looking all over for you," Paisley said, giving Levi an exasperated eye roll when she found him in the barn.

"Sorry," he said, setting the manure fork aside as he straightened. "What's up?"

She quirked an eyebrow. "Mucking out stalls on Christmas, huh? You must really be missing her."

He gave a small nod, not wanting to go into it with Paisley. He'd already told one sibling what had happened, and that was enough.

She gave him a sympathetic frown. "I'm sorry you didn't get a chance to say goodbye to her. I would have stalled if I could have."

"It's okay," he said, turning back to clean out the stall.

"You took off so fast after everyone opened gifts that I didn't get a chance to give this to you."

He turned, noticing for the first time the wrapped gift she carried. It was flat and slightly rectangular. He tilted his head. "You didn't draw my name this year." They always drew names for the sibling gift exchange, and he'd gotten a Leatherman tool from Alex already.

She shook her head, extending the gift to him. "It's not from me. Rachel left it for you."

His stomach dropped. "Oh. Thanks." He accepted the gift, debating what to do before setting it down on a nearby stool.

"You're not even going to open it?" Paisley asked.

"I'm … saving it for later," he answered lamely. He didn't want to open it in front of his sister. She'd always had that uncanny twin sense of reading his thoughts based on his expression.

She folded her arms, staring him down. "Okay, spill it."

He picked up the fork and started shoveling again. "Spill what?" He faced away from her to hide his expression.

She groaned in frustration. "I cannot believe you told Garrett what happened instead of me."

Levi froze. He slowly turned to face her. "He *told* you?"

She scoffed, waving a hand. "Of course. It's Garrett."

His throat moved. "I asked him not to say anything."

"According to Garrett, you told him to swear to not tell anyone, but he never agreed to that before you came out with the whole story. So he claims he didn't break your confidence."

Levi shook his head. He was going to strangle his brother.

Paisley crossed her arms. "Whatever happened to our twin pact? Your supposed to tell me things—and this is big."

"You were baiting me to see if I would confide in you?" He narrowed his eyes.

She raised her hands. "It was a test, yes. And I admit I'm a little hurt you didn't tell me." She frowned.

Levi blew out a deep breath, his frustration ebbing away. He could never stay angry at Paisley for long, and he understood where she was coming from. He would have been hurt if the situation was reversed and she didn't tell him. "Sorry." He rested his hands on the handle of the rake. "I would have said something eventually. I'm just still trying to process it myself. I only saw the text last night."

"I get it." She paused, scuffing her boot in the dirt. "But we all think you should talk to her about it."

He stared, dumbfounded. "What do you mean, '*We all?*' Who else did Garrett tell?"

She lifted a shoulder. "Everyone."

"Everyone?" Levi groaned. "Unbelievable!" He ran a hand over his face. "I ask him not to say anything and he goes and tells the whole family." He made a fist, ready to find his brother and wrestle him into a headlock.

"Don't be mad," Paisley pleaded. "Everyone noticed how solemn you were while we opened gifts this afternoon, and Mom was the first one to make a comment after you left. She assumed you missed Rachel, and the rest of us piped in about it until Garrett finally set us straight." She touched his shoulder. "I'm so sorry, Levi. We were all shocked about it. For her to be hiding something like that … I don't know." She shook her head. "It just doesn't seem like the Rachel we knew."

"Yeah." He scoffed, his throat tightening as he turned away, resuming his work with more force than necessary. "It surprised me too."

"Is there anything I can do?" Paisley hedged.

"Thanks, but for now I just want to be alone."

"Okay." She paused. "I'll make sure we save some of Mom's chocolate trifle for you."

"Thanks, Pais." He gave her a brief smile and then turned back to his task.

She left the barn and Levi finished cleaning the stall and washed up. He looked around the barn, wondering what else could be done, but there wasn't anything urgent. He stepped over to Cal's stall and his horse came over, greeting him with a friendly nicker as Levi fed him a handful of oats.

"What do you say, boy? Should I open it or leave it be?" he asked as conflicting emotions warred in his chest. He itched to know what Rachel had gotten him or when she'd found the time, but on the other hand, he wasn't sure he wanted to deal with the emotions a gift from her would bring.

Cal finished the handful of oats, sniffing for more before tossing his head. Levi sighed, giving his horse a wry smile. "I'll take that as a yes." He walked over to the stool where he'd left the package and carefully tore open the wrapping paper. His heart hitched. It was a framed black and white picture of his great-grandfather's cabin—the place where they'd first confessed their feelings for each other.

A rush of emotion clogged his throat but he fought against it. He wanted to send Rachel a text to thank her for the thoughtful gift, but he couldn't afford to open the channel of communication with her again. He fingered the frame, admiring the professional photograph.

"Thanks, Rachel," he said quietly. "I wish you all the best." And he meant it. As much as her dishonesty had cost him, he still wanted her to be happy. Hopefully she would forgive him for not keeping in touch ... or maybe she was already forgetting about him. He wished he could do the same. The pain in his chest intensified and he knew it would be a long time before he could forget about Rachel Hartman ... a very, very long time.

CHAPTER 21

"Alright, I think that just about wraps it up," Rachel said, thanking the small family she'd just finished photographing. "I'll get the files to you as soon as possible, and I think you're going to like them."

"I know we will," the mom said, smiling wide as she gave Rachel a spontaneous hug. "Thanks so much. I've always wanted to do an outdoors photo shoot, and the desert is the perfect backdrop."

"It really is stunning," Rachel agreed. "This is one of my favorite spots to do photo shoots. Can you guys find your way back to the city alright, or do you need directions?"

"We'll be fine," the husband answered. "GPS for the win." He held up his cell and then waved at her as his wife shepherded their two rambunctious boys back to their car.

Rachel waved and then stowed her camera in its case before heading to her own car. It was a pleasant evening and she considered staying to take pictures of the sunset, but then decided against it. Ever since she'd returned home from Montana, she'd lost her drive to do any extra photography beyond the work she was hired for.

It had been over three weeks since she'd gotten that last text from

Levi. She'd finally tried calling him the day after Christmas—and the next day after that. Her heart cracked and slowly shattered when she realized he wasn't going to call her back. That he'd been pretending to return her feelings when all along she'd been nothing more than a temporary guest he'd been assigned to help for a few days. The realization cut deep; so deep it hurt to breathe at times.

She'd spent hours editing the pictures and videos for Canyon Creek, highlighting the activities, rooms and amenities at the ranch. She also included shots emphasizing the fact that while guests were there, they were treated as family. She suggested that idea as a potential slogan for Canyon Creek in her email, and then sent all of the files to Garrett and Claire.

Claire emailed back shortly after with effusive praise for Rachel's work and sent her a generous tip in addition to the already generous pay. While she was polite, there wasn't any more mention of hoping that Rachel could come back for a visit. She'd gotten the same reaction from Paisley when she'd sent Hannah's baby pictures. Paisley had expressed heartfelt thanks in her email and had even sent a lovely gift basket as a thank you but said nothing about hoping to see Rachel again. The change was so noticeable that Rachel almost wondered if Levi had started dating someone else. It was the only explanation she could think of for Levi's silence and Claire and Paisley's reticence. Garrett didn't reply at all.

The idea of Levi dating someone else crushed her. She'd soaked her pillow with tears every night for a week straight, wondering how she could have been so wrong about his feelings for her. She even felt bad enough about the way he'd ignored her phone calls that she'd reached out to apologize to Mark for not returning his calls. She wasn't interested in a relationship with him of course, but now she knew what it felt like to be ignored and she vowed never to do that to anyone again. He was already dating someone else and smugly accepted her apology. It helped ease her guilt about ignoring him, but it didn't ease the pain of her broken heart over Levi.

If only he would send her a simple text to let her know he wasn't interested, it would hurt less than the silence. Apparently, the Davis family treated their guests like family, but as soon as they left, they got the cold shoulder.

Rachel climbed into her car with a sigh. She headed away from the desert and back toward the city, turning on some music as a distraction when her phone rang. Sage's face flashed on the screen and she swiped to answer the call. "Hey, Sage. What's up?"

"Are you done with that photo shoot you had tonight?" Sage asked.

"I just finished a little bit ago. Why?"

"Can you meet me at Encanto Park? I need to talk to you."

Rachel frowned, noting the hint of anxiety in her friend's voice. "Is everything okay?"

"Yes, it's fine. I just have to talk to you, and it's something I'd rather tell you in person."

"O-okay," Rachel said, curious what could be so important that her best friend couldn't just tell her over the phone. "I can be there in twenty minutes."

"I'll be waiting."

The call dropped and Rachel mused over what Sage might want to tell her. She'd only been dating her boyfriend Brice for a few months, so it couldn't be engagement news, could it? Or maybe they'd gotten in a fight and Sage just need someone to talk to—but she hadn't sounded sad. *Hmm.*

Rachel pulled into a parking space at the downtown Phoenix park that had been one of their favorite hangouts when they were younger. She found Sage sitting and watching the sunset at their usual spot on the grass near the lake. "I am dying of curiosity," Rachel said. She sat down next to her friend and searched her face for clues. "Is this good news or bad news?"

Sage nodded. "Good. Definitely good." Her eyes sparkled with excitement. "You'll never guess who I talked to yesterday."

"Um?" Rachel scrunched her brow in thought. Sage had called her here to tell her she'd talked to someone? She was something of a fangirl when it came to movie stars, but she knew Rachel wasn't really into keeping up with Hollywood. "Was it a celebrity or something?" she guessed.

"Basically." Sage moved to her knees, bouncing up and down. "Hope Sullivan!" She waved a hand. "I mean, I guess she's Hope Davis now, but you know who I'm talking about. "

"Oh." Rachel's heart hiccupped at the mention of Hope. She'd completely forgotten that she'd given her number to Sage. Thinking of Hope caused a fresh sting in her chest. "That's awesome," she said, trying to match Sage's enthusiasm. "What did you guys talk about?"

"Well of course I was super nervous. It took me forever to work up the courage to call her, and I couldn't stop gushing about how much I love her yoga channel, but she was *so* nice. I knew she would be. She's always so sweet in her videos." Sage clasped her hands, her eyes dreamy. "I still can't believe you got to meet her in person."

Rachel smiled. "I'm glad you got to talk to her. She really is sweet." She bit the inside of her cheek. She'd thought Hope and Paisley and the others would become her good friends, but that clearly wasn't going to be the case.

Sage nodded and then leaned forward, touching her knee as her expression grew serious. "Yoga wasn't the only thing we talked about though."

The air rushed from Rachel's lungs. "It wasn't?" she managed.

Sage shook her head. "We also talked about Levi." She watched for her reaction.

Rachel went completely still, her heart pounding in her ears. "What did Hope say?"

"She asked me how you were doing, and I told her the truth." She shrugged. "I said you were really hurting over Levi."

Rachel nodded, unable to speak. Sage always had her back so she wasn't surprised she would do some investigating on her behalf. She held her breath as she waited for her to continue.

Sage shifted, leveling her with a gaze. "Hope told me that Levi was hurting too."

She blinked. "That can't be true. Did you tell her I tried calling him and he hasn't called me back?"

"Yes. And I found out why." She raised both eyebrows. "You're not going to believe this."

"Tell me!" Rachel burst out, grabbing her wrists.

Sage kept a hold of her arms. "The night that you guys went on a sleigh ride ... Christmas Eve, right?"

Rachel nodded impatiently, waiting for her to go on.

"Well, it sounds like you left your phone in Levi's coat ... I'm not even going to ask about why you had his coat, though I *am* curious," she raised her eyebrows.

"Sage!" Rachel pleaded.

"Sorry." She straightened and continued, "Anyway, Levi found your phone in his coat and saw that text from Mark—the one you told me about before you blocked him."

Rachel's stomach dropped.

Sage's face scrunched together. "He totally thought you'd been lying to him and that Mark was your boyfriend."

"No. *No!*" Rachel jumped up and fisted her hands in her hair. "*Ugh,* that stupid text. I can't believe this. If only I'd blocked Mark sooner." She dropped her hands, wringing them together as her thoughts raced. "Why didn't Levi say anything to me? He totally acted like he didn't realize my phone was in his pocket. This whole thing could have been avoided if he'd said something."

"I was scared to."

Rachel's heart stopped. She turned at the sound of Levi's voice behind her and her mouth fell open. He was here. Standing right in front of her. His brown eyes were tight with apology as he held his cowboy hat in his hands.

"W-what are you doing here?" she stammered.

He shook his head, locking onto her gaze. "I had to see you." He took a slight step closer. "When I realized what an idiot I'd been jumping to conclusions, I had to apologize in person. Hope got me in touch with Sage and she helped me out."

Sage touched her elbow. "I'm sorry I kept it a secret. I figured you two had some sorting out to do, and Levi was afraid you wouldn't want to see him so we came up with a plan." She gave Rachel a sidearmed hug. "I'm going to take off now so you guys can talk. Call me later, okay?"

"Okay," Rachel answered numbly, still too shocked to form coherent thought.

Sage gave her another squeeze and then dropped her arm, nodding at Levi. "Good luck," she said.

"Thanks for all of your help." He dipped his chin at her and Sage gave Rachel a loaded side glance before she walked away.

Levi cleared his throat and turned to Rachel, his expression lined with regret. "I don't blame you if you won't forgive me. I should have told you when I saw the text." He ran a hand along the back of his neck. "I just couldn't see past the hurt and betrayal I felt, and I acted like a complete fool. It killed me not to answer your texts or call you back after you left ... I should have." He dropped his hand and searched her face. "I just didn't want to have it confirmed that the girl I'd fallen in love with was already taken."

Rachel's heart climbed into her throat. "The girl you fell in love with?" she repeated softly.

He nodded, taking another small step forward as he held her gaze. "Head over heels." He reached for her hand, sending an electric current straight up her arm. "Can you forgive me, Rachel?"

She blinked slowly. "I wasn't dating anyone," she explained. "I'd broken up with Mark before I left for Montana. He kept calling me and then sent that text. I've blocked him now, but it was all a misunderstanding."

"I know. Hope told me everything." He tilted her chin up to look at him. "I am *so* sorry. I promise that from now on I'll always be upfront and open with you about anything I have a question about."

A small, excited shiver ran through her at his reference to their future. "What makes you think there'll be a 'from now on' between us?" she asked, folding her arms and arching an eyebrow.

"I'm hoping there will be." His gaze pleaded with her. "I'm willing to do whatever it takes to earn a second chance."

"Anything?" she asked, pursing her lips.

"Anything." His expression was earnest.

She frowned and took a step back, conflicted. Part of her wanted to be mad at him for how deeply he'd hurt her. She wanted him to know how many tears she'd shed that could have been avoided if he'd simply asked her about the text. But he'd already apologized for all of that, and she'd never been good at holding a grudge … how could she, with this handsome cowboy facing her with his hat in his hands? She tapped her chin, letting a few seconds pass before she blew out a breath. "Okay. How about taking me to dinner? I'm starving."

His face went slack and his eyes filled with relief. "Deal." He stepped toward her, wrapping his arms around her and pulling her in for a tight hug. Rachel melted into him, her entire body filled with joy as she held onto Levi, never wanting to let go. They didn't speak for several moments, lost in the magnitude of the moment before he pulled back, gently caressing the sides of her face before pressing his lips to hers.

Rachel's knees went weak. She wrapped her arms firmly around his waist, drawing him closer as she kissed him back, her heart floating in her chest as her world fell into place. She no longer wanted to be wild and free; she wanted to belong with Levi. Safe and secure, where she belonged.

After several long seconds she pulled away, searching his face as she played with the hair at the base of his neck. She smiled coyly when she felt the goosebumps on his skin at her touch. "By the way," she said softly. "That girl you fell in love with?"

He nodded, pressing his forehead to hers.

"She's in love with you too."

His eyes filled with wonder. "In that case," his voice was slightly husky as his mouth tipped up in one corner. "I think she'd better get used to wearing this." He set his cowboy hat gently on her head and nodded in satisfaction. "It looks good on you."

She smiled and tilted her face up at him. "I think I was meant to be a cowgirl."

"I think you were meant to be *my* cowgirl."

Her heart fluttered. "Agreed." She slipped her hand into his. "I'll go wherever you want me to, cowboy."

"And I can be happy anywhere too ... as long as I'm with you." Levi leaned down to give her one more sweet, achingly soft kiss.

Rachel's heart threatened to burst as she wrapped her arms around his neck, savoring the warmth of his kiss. It had come a few weeks late, but now there wasn't a doubt in her mind—Christmas miracles really did exist.

EPILOGUE

"$\mathcal{I}$'m at a loss," Rachel admitted, holding her camera up to frame a shot of the brilliant fall leaves on the trees bordering Crescent Lake. She took a few pictures and lowered the camera with a contented sigh.

"At a loss for what?" Levi asked with an amused smile.

She turned and took a picture of Cal and Juniper, the horses they'd ridden which were grazing nearby, and then lowered her camera with another sigh. "I've been to Canyon Creek in all four seasons now, and I'm still at a complete loss as to which is my favorite. I don't think I'll ever be able to decide." She and Levi had taken turns visiting each other as often as they could manage it for nearly a year, but each time she had to leave the ranch she was always sad to go. As much as she liked Phoenix, it didn't sing to her soul the way Montana did.

"Huh. That is quite a dilemma," Levi said with a teasing glimmer in his eyes.

"It really is. I feel like I should have a definite favorite, you know? But when each season offers something unique and gorgeous, how can I be expected to settle on just one?" She gave him a playful frown and looked down at her camera to adjust the settings. Her landscape pictures had grown increasingly popular on her website and the prints she sold were quickly becoming her main source of income. It was a win-win because it meant she could write off her frequent visits to Montana—and Levi was always more than willing to be her guide, showing her new mountains, rivers, and lakes to photograph. She'd even been able to capture several shots of wildlife and was thrilled with the variety of wild animals in the rugged terrain.

"You know, we're not too far from my property," Levi said casually. "How would you feel about riding over there?"

She brightened. "I'd love it." He'd taken her to his property last spring but they hadn't visited it since then. She knew he was eager to have his own place, but now that he had his own herd of cattle to look after and some acres of land to farm, he was busier than ever.

"I don't know if Garrett has already talked to you about this, but there's a problem with the website for the ranch," Levi said after they mounted their horses and he pulled up next to her on Cal.

She frowned. "He hasn't said anything. What's going on?"

"The problem is that the pictures you took were so darn amazing, we're constantly overbooked." He gave her a sly wink.

She laughed. "I have noticed how busy it's been … but if I'm being completely honest, I like that the rooms are all booked." She glanced at him sideways. "That way I have an excuse to sleep in the spare bedroom in your parents' house instead of in a cabin. It's nice to be closer to you."

"I agree." He gave her a rakish grin, holding her gaze for a moment before he faced forward, nodding ahead. "There it is."

Rachel followed his line of sight and gasped. "What is that?"

He laughed. "It's a house."

"But it's on your property." It was the most charming house she'd ever seen, painted a lovely shade of blue with two stories and a wrap-around porch in the front. It was exactly the kind of house she would have built if she could choose. In fact … it was exactly the style of house she'd pointed out months ago when her mom had been looking at houses in magazines, asking Rachel what her dream house would look like if she could choose. Her mom had always been interested in home design, so Rachel hadn't thought anything of it—until now. She turned and gaped at Levi. "You built a house and didn't tell me about it?"

He shrugged, his eyes glowing in delight. "I wanted it to be a surprise."

She shook her head slowly. "It certainly is." They rode the horses up closer and dismounted. Rachel was still too stunned to process that the gorgeous house in front of her belonged to Levi. "I can't believe this," she said, turning to face him.

"Do you like it?" His eyes were tight as he searched her face.

"It's absolutely perfect." She turned to admire the front of the house again. There were even flower boxes beneath the lower windows and darling black shutters on the sides. She swallowed as tears welled up in her eyes. It couldn't be a coincidence. It was exactly the way she'd described her dream house to her mom.

"Good." Levi took both of her hands in his, facing her toward him as he looked deep into her eyes. "Because I have an idea about your dilemma over which season is your favorite." He brushed a stray strand of hair from her cheek.

She nodded slowly, too emotional to speak.

His mouth turned up in the corner. "What if you didn't have to choose one? What if you could stay here—with me—and spend a life-time deciding which was your favorite?"

"Levi," she whispered, her body trembling in anticipation as a tear slid down her cheek.

He brushed it away, capturing her gaze as he reached into his pocket and slowly got down on one knee, holding up a glittering diamond ring. "Rachel Hartman, will you marry me?"

Her tears flowed freely as she covered her mouth with her hands and nodded. "Levi, you know the answer is yes," she breathed, smiling so big her cheeks hurt as he stood and swept her into his arms.

"I love you, Rachel," he said, pressing his mouth against her hair.

"I love you too." She held onto him, desperate to keep him close and never let go.

"The inside of the house isn't finished yet," he explained. "I wanted you to be able to make it your own, however you like it." He pulled back and smiled. "I can't wait to carry you across the threshold."

"I can't wait either. Let's get married today," she teased ... though not completely kidding. She would marry him in a heartbeat, but her mom would never forgive her if they eloped.

"Don't tempt me," he said, tilting her chin up.

She wrapped her arms around his neck, searching his eyes as her heart thrummed in her chest. "I know it's only a few months away, but I would love a Christmas wedding. I don't want anything big or grand so I think we could pull it off." She paused and gave him an impish smile. "And maybe if we're lucky, we'll get snowed in on our honeymoon."

He chuckled, the sound deep and rumbling in his chest as he pulled her closer. "I could definitely get on board with that."

"Me too." She tipped her face up to his. "Being snowed in with my cowboy sounds good to me."

He smiled and tipped the edge of his hat before pressing his lips to hers in a spine-tingling, heart-melting kiss.

LIKE THE BOOK?

Please consider leaving a review on Amazon, it's the best way to say thank you to an author.
Thank you so much!

GET A FREE BOOK!

Join Holly's VIP List today for sneak peeks, news on the latest releases, and FREE books!

www.authorhollystevenson.com

ALSO BY HOLLY STEVENSON

ABOUT THE AUTHOR

Holly Stevenson is a romantic at heart. She loves to read, eat out, watch movies, and spend time with family and friends. As a former flight attendant, she has plenty of traveling hours under her belt, but never tires of exploring new places. One of her favorite pastimes is researching potential vacation spots.

Holly also enjoys being near water, and has a weakness for any combination of chocolate and caramel. She rarely sleeps in, preferring the early morning quiet to accommodate her incurable writing addiction. She is blessed to live with her favorite people: her husband and four kids, in a house overlooking the beautiful Rocky Mountains.

To learn more about Holly, and to get her FREE book, please visit her website: www.authorhollystevenson.com

Made in the USA
Monee, IL
18 February 2021